P A.W.

It

QUEEN'S CACHE

An Evans Novel of Romance

QUEEN'S CACHE

BETH HENDERSON

M. EVANS & COMPANY, INC.   NEW YORK

Library of Congress Cataloging-in-Publication Data

Henderson, Beth.
Queen's cache / Beth Henderson.
p.   cm.—(An Evans novel of romance)
ISBN 0-87131-650-1 : $16.95
I. Title   II. Series.
PS3558.E4823Q44   1991
813.54—dc20   91-21403
                    CIP

M. Evans and Company, Inc.
216 East 49th Street
New York, New York 10017

Manufactured in the United States of America

9 8 7 6 5 4 3 2 1

To my parents,
Bob and Mary Daniels,
who first introduced me
to the joys of pencil and paper.

Prologue

10TH CENTURY B.C., Kingdom of Saba, Arabian Peninsula.

The mukarrib, the priest-ruler, stood silently at the artisan's side watching as the final strokes fell, completing the plaque. Crafted of purest gold, the slate was a fitting tribute to a once prosperous reign. The carefully etched characters carried both praises for the queen and warnings to those who would disturb her rest. Soon it would serve as a seal on her tomb.

She had been a great ruler pleasing the people of Saba with both her beauty and her wisdom. She had brought her subjects prosperity through the opening of a trade route with the northern kingdoms. Now she lay at rest. The light had gone out of the land and out of the mukarrib's life. The treasure he had collected and placed around her would have to suffice as a memorial to her glory.

A final flourish of the artisan's tool completed his work. He leaned back to admire the panel, his eyes carefully following each of the parallel lines and geometric designs of script, checking that all was as perfect as it must be for a queen of Saba.

The workman looked to his lord, the mukarrib, for approval. In contrast to the artisan's simple white robe, the priest was resplendent in garments that proclaimed his high station. The cloth was silken and whispered with a sound like the sigh of a dove when he moved. The robe was embroidered with a design of silver bulls, the symbol of the moon god over whose temple the priest presided. Beautifully crafted silver cuffs clasped the mukarrib's wrists and accented the

1

long, elegant shape of his hands. Even his sandals were ornamented with wrought silver.

When the great man nodded, the artisan gave a soft sigh of relief and turned back to admire his creation one last time. The sigh became a gasp for air as a knotted cord encircled his neck. It tightened as the mukarrib twisted the weapon, expertly closing his servant's windpipe.

Mountain sunshine poured through the palace windows, bathing the body of the dying man. Golden beams caught the gilt edges of the finished plaque, creating a fire-like brilliance along the etched letters that made up the queen's name. Bilqis.

The mukarrib watched the dust motes dance in the beam as his victim's struggles subsided. When the artisan had ceased to twitch, the priest allowed the body to slip quietly to the floor. With quiet, precise movements, the mukarrib rewound the cord about the waist of his robes, then picked up the golden plaque and left the room. Behind him the sun inched its way higher in a perfect blue sky, leaving the crumbled body of the artisan in shadow, forgotten now by both ruler and elements.

The journey to the tomb was not far. Mourning for the queen could not halt the seasons, and the mukarrib passed people in the fields. If they looked after their priest-ruler curiously, he did not see. His step quickened as he climbed higher into the mountainous terrain.

The people feared him, and it was well that they did so. No one would try to follow him. His plans had been so swiftly executed that even his enemies would be thwarted. They would never find the last resting place of Queen Bilqis. They would never find him. Comforting as the thought was, it could not bring a smile to his harsh face. Only his reunion with his queen would cheer his soul now.

He climbed ever higher on the mountain. Once he paused to rest, to turn his face to the east and breathe the dry air of the Rub' Al-Khali Desert, the land of his birth. To the west rose the impressive and cool heights of Nabi Shu'ayb, the mountain whose beauty had been so pleasing to Bilqis. Her windows in the palace opened on the vista. He had often found her lost in contemplation of the landscape. Even at night Bilqis had thought the sight beautiful as 'Awwam, the moon god cloaked the crags in a silver light. She would turn to her mukarrib, the lunar glow spilling over her sleek raven hair, over her chin, clinging robe, and beg him to help her celebrate the glory of 'Awwam. The sight of her skin, fair as peeled almonds, and her mouth, as cooling to taste and feel as a grape, had never failed to move him. Her wish was his wish. Together they had built a temple to worship her favored deity. Now she was gone.

The mukarrib turned away from the view and made his way to the tomb. He had traveled widely in his queen's service. Had accompanied her on her journey north to visit the monarch who worshipped but one god. Had sailed to the land of many gods and of men who were god-kings, the pharaohs. His memorial to her was a combination of all the things he had seen as well as those dear to the tradition of the kingdom of Saba.

He stood for a long moment surveying the landscape, looking for unwanted eyes. When he was satisfied that he was alone, the priest-ruler moved to the cliff face and lowered himself to the nearly hidden outcropping of rock a short drop below. The ledge itself widened as the rock dipped back into the mountain, weathered into a hollow by the wind. Further back in the aperture, the mukarrib bent low and entered a man-made chamber in the rock. The men he had left on guard lay in awkward positions, their eyes sightless now. Empty goblets lay near each, evidence that they had drunk to the queen's memory, quenching their thirst from the wine. He doubted they had even noticed the faint taste of almonds, the only sign that he had poisoned the jar.

Stepping over them he moved to the inner door of the tomb and placed the plaque in position, both sealing and honoring the queen's resting place. The entrance chamber was narrow and devoid of ornamentation along its walls. In Egyptian tombs, highly colored figures marched in processions recounting the glories of the royal personage they honored. For Bilqis there were no paintings on the stone. The chamber was as stark as the feeling of loss in the mukarrib's heart. The wealth that his queen took with her in death was arranged around her body in the inner room. The larger doorway had been filled in when the last of the caravan goods was in place. Silks, spices, precious stones, wines, her favorite delicacies, all kept her company now. Just as the soldiers continued to guard her even in death. Just as he, in the end, would stay as well.

He retrieved the goblets, placing them in a neat row. He straightened the helmet of one dead guard, adjusted the robe of another. When at last he was satisfied, the mukarrib went to the entrance of the tomb and released one last mechanism.

He smiled when the first rumblings of the small avalanche reached him. He moved back from the entrance to sit in the only piece of furniture in the outer room, an ornately carved throne room chair. From his position just before the door to Bilqis's chamber, the mukarrib watched rubble spill over the opening. Dust swelled into his tomb. He held an elaborately decorated piece of cloth to his mouth to avoid choking, his actions calm and deliberate. As the last of the sun-filled world disappeared from his sight, the mukarrib, priest-ruler and lover of the queen of Saba, closed his eyes and waited to join his beloved in death.

Chapter One

NORTH YEMEN (SAN'A'), Arabian Peninsula, early July, 1990.

In spite of its antiseptic appearance, the hospital emergency room smelled of death—his death, Badr al-Hashid thought.

The shutters were closed tightly against the noonday sun but his eyes were shut even tighter as he fought the pain. He couldn't hear the prayer call although he knew the voices of the holy men filled the city of San'a' with their cries. The pounding in his mind shut out reality. It was not Allah who was part of this world of pain. Pain was the realm of Shaitan.

A soft hand touched his sweat-dampened forehead. At first he though it was that of his wife, Sikina, brushing his hair back as she had often done early in their marriage. But the hand moved on, prying his eyelid open to shine a pencil thin beam of light into his dilated pupil. When the light was taken away, Badr felt the pressure of cool fingers on his wrist.

"What happened?" a distant male voice asked in English. It was as cold and impersonal as the hands had been.

"*Ar-kalb a kilaab* nearly ran him over in the street," a gruff-voiced man answered. The Arabian curse flowed more easily from his lips than the English words. "But it wasn't the dog of a driver in the jeep who nearly killed him. He was stabbed. The knife sliced along his ribs."

"Mmm," the first voice mused. Badr felt probing fingers along his left side. "We'll need x-rays. Any identification? Oh, I see.

5

Yes. Then you've notified his relatives?"

Badr tried to concentrate. What had he been doing? Where had he been? Why would anyone try to kill him?

Then he remembered.

The ancient Arab quarter of the city had been blacker than the robes of any Islamic woman and just as enveloping. Nahar, the thief, had insisted that they meet in the heart of the night, the only time they could be sure they were unseen.

The air had cooled somewhat even in the *suq*, the marketplace. The twisted puzzle of winding lanes, many as wide as a man was tall but most as close as a coffin, were unfathomable to Badr in daylight. Perhaps he should have refused to concede to Nahar's wishes. The man had worked for him on a dig only once. It had been before Badr learned of the man's preferred "trade." It was his honor as a respected archaeologist that had forced Badr to expel the man Nahar from the camp. But it was his obsession, his all-consuming passion to unearth evidence on the existence of the Queen of Saba that made it necessary to use Nahar's specialized talents. It was as if their meeting was ordained, kismet.

The fates had been right. Nahar had found a key to the location of a tomb. He, Dr. Badr ibn Yussuf al-Hashid, had held an artifact, a part of ancient Saba, in his hands and known the the fortune and acclaim for such a find would soon be his.

The plaque Nahar had brought him at his house was not uncommon in shape for a 10th century B.C. artifact. What made it unique was the fact that it was crafted of gold and inscribed with the equally golden name of a queen. Bilqis.

His hands had sweat upon reading her name. His heart had pounded so loudly in his ears that he could barely hear what Nahar told him. Quickly his eyes had scanned the stiff symbols of the Sabaean script. They weren't flowing and free like modern Arabic. The upright lines, connected triangles, the linked or divided circles, and forked designs held no secrets from Badr. His reputation as an epigraphist of Sabaean inscriptions had been made early in his career. He read the etched letters nearly as easily as he read the Koran, and far more eagerly.

She was there. The queen of ancient Saba. Her legends had traveled far and been recounted in scripture and through word-of-mouth. Bilqis, builder of temples, promoter of commerce, ambassador-queen of the ancient world.

"There is more?" he had asked Nadar.

"Much more," the thief had promised and grinned widely. His teeth were blackened or missing. His breath smelled of ghat.

Badr had no use for the euphoric feeling produced from chewing the tender leaves of the ghat bush. He was sure Nahar frequently indulged in the substance. In all probability the thief spent his days stuffing his cheeks with ghat leaves, then washing the residue down his throat with water. His eyes had the look of an addict, the pupils shrunken to the size of pebbles. To Badr the excitement of an archaeological find was a stimulant. And to unearth the legendary Bilqis, Queen of Saba, would be the ultimate high.

He had paid Nahar the sum asked for the plaque, then had hidden it away. The meeting in the old city a week later had been but the next step toward immortality. Nahar had given him the location of the tomb in exchange for a ridiculously low amount.

They had met in the heart of the *suq*. The shops of the vendors were empty at that time of night. The flimsy wooden awnings that protected their open fronts created illusionary caverns along the base of the multi-storied stone houses. Only a few scavenger rats prowled the lane. Or so Badr had thought.

The shadow had materialized before him on the street. A stray beam of moonlight had glinted on the smooth surface of the attacker's *jambiya* as he raised it against Badr. The dagger had descended in a flash, driving into Badr's flesh. Just as swiftly, it was withdrawn, leaving pain and a warm dampness in its stead. Badr had gasped in shock, his hand going to his side and finding it already sticky with his own blood. When he looked back at his attacker, the shadow had melted back into the maze of narrow alleys.

Badr tried hard to remember something of his enemy of the night before. But the concealing draperies of night cloaked the shadowy figure. He thought the shape had been almost childlike, yet it loomed large in his imagination.

His memory slipped away as the pain recalled his attention. It was no use fretting over the incident. The knowledge he carried was safe in his mind where no thief could touch it. The weak link in the chain was the existence of the map. It led to the clever compartment in the old house in Sirwah where he had hidden the golden plaque. Only his cousin Hadi knew of the cache's existence, and he was in the United States, thousands of miles away from the site. He wondered if Hadi even carried his portion of the map all these years later. Badr kept his own share as a reminder of that one particular summer. It was impossible to tell with Hadi, though. The man lived in two worlds and was uncomfortable in each.

"Dr. Faraday?"

The voice was soft and seemed to come from afar. Badr stiffened at its sound.

"I've come to see my husband," the voice continued.

"Just a moment more, please," the doctor murmured.

Badr strugged to sit up and was pushed gently back onto the table by two pairs of hands. He forced his eyes open to stare at the white-coated men gathered around him. Focusing on the tall redheaded man with the stethoscope dangling around his neck, Badr spat his wife's name. "Sikina. *Qahba.*"

Dr. Eliot Faraday clucked his tongue. "A slut, is she?" He knew it was the custom among Arabian couples not to show their affection. The more a husband shunned a wife the more he convinced his friends that he was besotted with her.

The man on the emergency room gurney was clearly a Sanarian of wealth. He wore the white robe of the Yemeni elite over flowing trousers but his footwear was of unmistakable Italian origin. The belt that gathered the now stained robe in at his waist was wide and covered with embroidery. He had either forsworn the cere-monial dagger and sheath of his class or it had been stolen as he lay unconscious in the *suq*. Even after a jeep had just missed running over his prone body, it had still been hours before Badr al-Hashid had been brought to the hospital ward. The man was lucky he hadn't bled to death in the market place!

Faraday detached a clipboard from its hook on the end of the bed. He would be glad to get back to the States where there were sufficient staff members to handle the details like paperwork. As a volunteer sent to train native physicians, Faraday found himself often forced to perform the duties of an orderly and a nurse as well as those of a surgeon.

"I will need a signature before we can proceed," he said wearily

8

in Arabic. "If your wife can sign the release..."

The injured man sucked in his breath in pain before answering. "She will do nothing for me."

Faraday's brow arched but his voice was as detached as before. "Insurance?"

Badr hissed a curse through clenched teeth.

"Sorry," Faraday said. "Bad joke I suppose. We'll need x-rays. Perhaps I should consult with your wife first, though. Her name is Sikina, did you say?"

This time Badr did not answer. Beads of sweat stood out on his forehead.

Faraday hung the clipboard in its accustomed place. "Get his wife," he snapped to his assistant. "I'm going to give him something for the pain."

He had turned back to his patient and was slowly forcing air bubbles from a syringe when the woman, Sikina, entered the room.

She was covered from head to foot in the all enveloping black cloak common to Islamic women. The lower portion of her face was hidden behind a veil. It fluttered as she sucked in her breath at the sight of her husband. Above the veil her eyes were large and luminous, dark and mysterious. They were eyes that made promises Islamic law forbade her from keeping with any man other than the one chosen by her father to be her husband.

And that man had called her a slut, Faraday mused. Interesting. And, considering his own intimate knowledge of Sikina, quite appropriate.

The doctor turned back to his patient, pushing the plunger of the syringe until morphine oozed from the needle. He motioned for the orderly to hold Badr still while he injected the drug into the man's arm.

Badr jerked once in response to the prick of the needle. His eyes had closed but now they opened to gaze in feverish dislike on the dark form of his wife.

As if drawn by his look, the woman moved from her pose in the doorway. She crossed the room silently, wafting the sweet scent of hibiscus blossoms in her path.

The drug was already making its way through Badr's body, replacing the pain with an unnatural inertia. Before his wits were part of the euphoria, Badr tried to concentrate. Who would want him dead? And why?

The dark-clothed woman drifted closer to the table. Her husband's raven black hair clung to his face, the damp tendrils curling tightly along his sweat-drenched brow. He had lost his turban. His swarthy skin had paled several shades. But the hatred in his dark eyes as well as the gentle rise and fall of his chest proved that he still lived.

"*Jowz juyzaan?* Husband? What is your wish?"

Her voice was lyrical and as soothing as the sound of a courtyard fountain after the heat of the desert. Did she know that he had proof of her unfaithfulness?

The numbness inched from Badr's arm, searching out his nerves and killing sensation in them one at a time. He could feel the drug's approach. It washed over him like the encroaching desert sand when driven before the wind.

Sikina touched his hand. Her touch was cool and detached.

Badr made an effort to remain conscious. Sikina would rejoice with his death. She prayed for forbidden fruits believing it was his will alone that bound her within the confines of *'ird*, the law by which men controlled the actions of their women. Sikina had shamed him already, although the knowledge of her deceit was yet his secret. Revenge would be his alone and he had planned to allow her to wonder and imagine the fate he would give her as a punishment for her unfaithfulness. Now he wanted a swifter sentence.

Conscious thought was nearly gone, but Badr made one last effort to avenge himself. His voice was a mere whisper. "I divorce you, I divorce you, I ..."

Sikina pushed away her veil, unmindful of the doctor and his assistant. "Shaitan claim you, Badr al-Hashid," she spat. Her voice was no longer that of a compliant wife.

His pain had been vanquished by the deadly path of the morphine. Badr's conscious mind gave way before its onslaught and he slept before he completed the third and final phrase that would free him from his wife.

Sikina stared across the broken body of her husband at the amused face of Dr. Eliot Faraday. "Will he live?" she asked.

Faraday shrugged his narrow shoulders. "If you wish him to. But you don't, do you, Sikina, *mahbuwb a iyn?*"

"Fool," she spat. "Don't call me beloved here." She pointed one long carefully manicured and accusing finger at the silent white-coated assistant. "What if that cur were to speak of it? Our lives would be forfeit."

The doctor's winged brows raised in rebuke, their dark reddish hue like a slash of ochre against his sun-burned skin.

Sikina's life most definitely would be lost according to the *'ird.* Bound by this custom, an unfaithful wife was a blemish on the honor of her family. It would fall to Sikina's male relatives to cleanse their reputation with her blood. He knew that Sikina tempted fate only because her closest male relative was a man of mixed blood who had not embraced Islam. Faraday had never bothered to discover if the quaint though barbaric *'ird* was formally written in the *Shari'ah,* the Islamic law. As an American he believed it was possible for him to plead ignorance of the local customs. Failing that, his position at the hospital would pull weight. It was financed through a non-profit organization determined to help third-world countries.

"Mohammad knows the risks," Faraday said of his assistant. "And the profits. He's greedy, aren't you Mohammad?"

The shorter, broader man grinned widely, displaying very white teeth against his full black beard.

Faraday turned back to the woman. "Have you discovered anything more about the treasure?" he asked.

Sikina glared and whirled away from the table where her husband lay comatose. Her black draperies floated around her like dark angel wings. "No, curse you. He carries the map with him. I haven't been able to take it without his knowing."

Faraday motioned to his assistant. Together they straightened Badr's curled body. Without a word, the doctor began to search the drugged man's clothing for pockets. Faraday found the prize in a money belt hidden beneath Badr's robe.

The map was brittle and yellowed with age. On one side faded ink flowed in a scrawl that was no longer distinguishable as a written language. Faraday wasted little time on it. He turned to the roughly sketched layout drawn on the reverse side. The original outline was faint, but someone had gone over it with a dark pen. The ink had smeared in places to a dark brown, but there was no disputing the fact that the lines were those of a map. Or more precisely, half a map. The page had been torn raggedly apart.

The doctor looked up, frowning at the woman. "Where's the rest of it?"

Rather than scrutinize the map with him, she was carefully counting the stack of American money that had also been in her husband's money belt. Before answering, Sikina folded the currency and tucked it in her voluminous robe. "Why do you think I would know of it? He considers me a possession, not an equal. Why do you think I hate him?"

Faraday stared at the map awhile longer. It looked like the rough layout of a village. The artist had not been worried about identifying his landmarks. He had not named anything on his sketch. Perhaps he had been in a hurry.

"Who else knows of the treasure?" Faraday demanded.

"The Treasure of the Unifier?" She rolled the sound on her tongue, enjoying the feel of it, then nodded as if she were royalty condescending to notice the request of a commoner. "My cousin, Hadi ibn Dawud al-Bakil. He and Badr played together when they were children."

"And just where is this cousin now?"

Sikina stared down at the sleeping, broken body of her husband. She smoothed the soiled fabric of his trousers. "How long will it be before my husband goes to Allah?"

Faraday swore under his breath. She was a ruthless bitch. Perhaps she always had been, even as the sensual little girl he'd once toyed with during a week on Long Island. Yet being with her was like manna in the wilderness to a man like him, condemned by circumstances to practice medicine far from the bedside of wealthy patients. One ethical slip had afforded one of Faraday's rivals the opportunity to blackmail him into joining the mission outpost in the Yemeni highlands. Now Sikina dangled the carrot of riches before his eyes. Wealth beyond imagination, she had whispered huskily in his ear. The treasure trove of ancient Arabian artifacts, when sold on the black market, would give them a fortune. Riches enough to dwarf the wealth of Ali Baba's find in the cave of the forty thieves, Sikina insisted. All that she required of Eliot Faraday was to make it possible for her to leave the world of the East. All he had to do was kill her husband.

Faraday snapped directions at the orderly and scribbled a few quick instructions on the clipboard. "Take him for x-rays." As the door swung closed on the retreating forms of Mohammad and the gurney on which lay the unconscious Badr, Faraday escorted the solemn, once again veiled Sikina into the waiting room. "There is no telling at this point. I need more information before I can diagnose his internal injuries." He paused, glanced at his chart then faced her once more. "It doesn't look good, though. There is a chance your husband won't live through the night."

From behind the concealment of her veil, Sikina smiled. Her voice was equally serious when she answered. "If it be Allah's will, so be it," she said, then added in a whisper. "My cousin Hadi is in Washington, D.C."

The valet parking attendant admired the shapely expanse of the young woman's black stockinged leg as she climbed out of the Mercedes. He wondered if she was a model on assignment in Washington or whether she was another of the jet-setters who had flown in for the Arabian reception. She was streamlined, a woman who would look great in jeans. The sight of her in the deceptively simple black evening dress, with its enticing split skirt, was enough to fuel his dreams for weeks to come. She had a wide, ready smile. She flashed it at him and tossed him the keys to her car. He nearly missed them.

Valentina Crosby didn't notice. She looked up at the brightly lighted entrance to the museum and frowned. "I've got a bad feeling about this," she said. Her chin length sweep of candy-colored brown hair swayed as she shook her head.

"You always have bad feelings about parties, Val," her grandmother soothed. Loretta Crosby smiled brightly as she accepted the help of a second parking attendant in getting out of the black sedan. It amused her to watch the way men behaved around her lovely grand-daughter. They tended to look mesmerized, though Valentina never noticed.

Loretta's elegant silver-gray evening gown rustled softly as she joined her granddaughter on the pavement. "You've always hated parties," Loretta said. "I think it stems from that horrible bout of the measles you contracted at Jenny Lee's birthday party when you were in the third grade."

Valentina continued to glare at the modern museum structure. Lights gleamed from the tall, narrow windows. Someone had even invested in spot lights. The beams swept the heavens in synchronized formation, one to the left, one to the right, then both swung back to cross like swords in a Wilkinson blade commercial before going their separate ways once more.

"I hate Jenny Lee," Valentina reminded her grandmother. "And it has nothing to do with getting the measles," she insisted. "She stole Tom Mercer from me in high school."

"He wasn't worth it, dear. And since Tom married her, I think the circle is complete. As I understand it, they loathe each other now."

Valentina laughed softly.

"Now do stop complaining, Val, and come enjoy yourself," Loretta instructed.

She took her granddaughter's arm and guided her along the red-carpeted walkway toward the museum entrance. Already she could hear the well-bred hum of conversation. It had taken a great deal of manipulation of Washington social strings for many of the guests to receive invitations to the reception for the visiting Arabian archaeologists. Loretta was sure that the fact that one of them was young and attractive had inspired many of the women to be present. In the weeks it had taken to unpack and arrange the exhibit, he had already acquired quite a following of Washington hostesses. Loretta wondered why the men had come, though. Could the visiting exhibition of Arabian artifacts be tied to the tensions in the Middle East? Located south of Saudi Arabia, Yemen was a small country with a wealth of ancient artifacts. Loretta patted her sleekly styled white hair and smiled at her willowy granddaughter. It didn't really matter if the exhibit was tied to politics or culture. Loretta had come, dragging the protesting Valentina along, for one reason only. She wanted to meet the young man who was causing such a stir in the hearts of Washington's female elite.

"You know I hate these things," Valentina said.

"But if you marry Todd, you'll spend the rest of your life attending political functions, dear. Think of this as a test."

Valentina sighed with undisguised disgust. "You said it again, Grandma. *If* I marry Todd. Since we've set the date I wish you'd admit defeat and accept him."

"You could do better."

"He's a good man."

"But not exciting, dear. I just wish you could be more like other young girls."

Valentina's eyes narrowed suspiciously. "And what does that cryptic remark mean?"

"Darling," Loretta cooed, and smiled brightly at a couple of her old cronies who were motioning for her to join them. Loretta merely waved at them. "It's almost the twenty-first century. Thus it is quite irregular, you know, for an engaged woman to live with her grandmother rather than her fiancé."

"Grandma!"

Loretta patted Valentina's arm complacently. "Don't look so shocked, Val. It's very simple. I don't want to see you get hurt. As much as I loved your grandfather, I never really knew the man until we shared the same roof."

Valentina thought fleetingly of the man she had know far too well, and the pain that closeness had caused. "I'm much happier with you," she declared.

"That, Val, is what I worry about," Loretta said. Sometimes it took a firm foot in the center of the back to push the chick from the nest.

Valentina had lived with her fond grandparents ever since her parents had been killed in the crash of a small plane nearly twenty years before. Loretta and Senator Graham Crosby had tried to fill the void. They'd taken Valentina with them, from Nevada to Washington, D.C., and back, following the political seasons. They had retired when their granddaughter had gone off to the University of Nevada, first in Reno, then transferring to the Las Vegas campus. The senator had died suddenly the year before. Valentina's return a few years earlier to the Washington house and her continued presence there had been a comfort to Loretta, who still expected to hear her husband's step on the stairs, or hear the booming sound of his voice in the next room.

"I know you are happy with me, dear," Loretta said. "But you really have no idea what kind of man you are planning to marry."

"Yes, I do," Valentina insisted. "If you'd take the time to talk to Todd, you wouldn't be so against him, Grandma. He's really wonderful."

Loretta sighed, unconvinced that Valentina knew what she was doing. Other women decried the ease with which young people fell into each other's beds. She really should be glad that her granddaughter wasn't one of them. But the problem was Todd McAllister. In her estimation, he was far from the right man for her Valentina. "Todd is so ... so correct in everything he does," Loretta complained.

They'd been over this before. Valentina had often thought that the constant repetition was enough to destroy her relationship with Todd. When she was with him she constantly looked for flashes of brilliance or dedication ... even a romantic look or phrase ... with which she could counter her grandmother's irrational dislike of him. She still hadn't found the golden gem that would change Loretta's mind.

Valentina tried one more time. "Todd has to be correct," she insisted. "He's in politics."

The attempt failed. "So was your grandfather," Loretta reminded, her tone still a bit militant. "But as least he had a sense of humor."

Valentina gave up. At least for the evening. Would her grandmother ever accept the man she had chosen as a bridegroom? She was beginning to doubt it. Instead she turned her attention to her surroundings, and the displays of artifacts.

The interior of the museum was stark and far too contemporary for Valentina's taste. It called out for an exhibition of modern paintings with splashes of uncoordinated color or perhaps a display of twisted but unidentifiable metal scultpures. It was not the place to host a collection of pre-Islamic archaeological treasures. The line of cases that held the artifacts were too pristine and homogeneous to house the remains of the ancient world. The program noted officiously that some of the pieces were from an era three millennia old. Now they stood under artistically arranged lights in sterile cases, a business card-sized identification plate at the side of each.

Loretta was greeted by a number of other guests as soon as they entered the main room. Although the reception had originally been planned to open the exhibit and honor the visiting team of archaeologists, the guests had little connection with the academic world. Senators rubbed shoulders with congressional pages. Private secretaries rubbed elbows with White House secretaries. Reporters watched and listened for any and all tidbits of gossip. Museum officials and university professors chatted with the robed and turbaned archaeologists from North Yemen, their eyes carefully following the trays of hors d'oeuvres carried through the crowd by waiters in short-jacketed tuxedos.

Valentina accepted a glass of champagne from the tray of a passing waiter and moved slowly down the row of cases. It had been a long time since she had allowed herself to even think of archaeology, much less visit a museum collection. She had cut herself off from that life. It was part of a young girl's dream but had no part in her current reality. She tried to tell herself the shaped pots with their curving rims, ibex and lion-shaped handles, and faded colors were just household utensils. Nothing more. But she could feel the old excitement in the pit of her stomach. If she wasn't careful, the embers would flare up once more. She couldn't afford a resurgence of interest in archaeology. The idea of piecing together a jigsaw puzzle of pottery sherds was a dream. And that dream was dead.

She had a new life now. One far away from the dusty ruins of an Anasazi Indian village. With Todd she would finally have a happily-ever-after. He had assured her there could be no other outcome to their marriage. It would be made in heaven.

Valentina sipped at her drink. Todd was so sure of himself and of her. She wished she could believe their life would be perfect. It would be, if she could only control the part of her that remembered another man and a love that had been both heaven and hell. Why did that feeling, the breathless anticipation, the rapid beating of her heart, appear so much better in retrospect than the comfortable future Todd represented?

She finished the champagne and returned the empty crystal to a waiter, declining another glass. Her answer wouldn't be easy to find. She only hoped it would all work out soon. Before the date of her wedding to Todd McAllister.

The broken pieces of an ibex figure lay in the case before her, the curved horns of the desert sheep reconstructed to show the graceful stylization of the period. Valentina's mind was caught in her own past, though. She had been an undergraduate majoring in anthropology. Harry Smith had been working on his masters in geology. He had swept her off her feet with his constant attentions. She had loved the feel of his coarse dark hair, the taste of his skin, and the burning intensity of his sky-bright eyes when he looked at her. She had adored him. And in return, Harry had hurt her.

"Valentina!"

The memories were gone swiftly, replaced by the numb acceptance that Valentina had developed through her more recent years on the Washington cocktail circuit. She turned at her grandmother's call, a polite smile already curving her lips.

Loretta had one of the guests of honor in tow. She dragged the dark-featured man by the arm. The white silk of his open robe floated back displaying a well-tailored dark suit, pale pink shirt and dark tie. The tie had a design of brighter pink splotches that from a distance looked like stylized circles. Thick black-brown hair curled from below the edge of his white turban. His smile was wide and as white as his native garments. It shone from beneath a curving dark mustache. A close-cut beard followed the contours of his jaw and joined the mustache to form a short goatee. With his sun-darkened skin and exotic costume he looked the embodiment of one of Scheherazade's dashing heroes.

Although he towered over her grandmother, Valentina knew he was just under six feet. She knew the curve of his lips, the light in his blue eyes. It had been five long years since she had run away from him. She was still running from the memories.

"There you are, darling," Loretta said coming to a breathless halt at her granddaughter's side. "I'd like you to meet Hadi ibn Dawud al-Bakil. He's one of the visiting archaeologists from North Yemen in Arabia." Loretta smiled up into the man's face. She was pleased to note his attention was all on Valentina. "Valentina is interested in archaeology," Loretta told him.

The man grinned at Valentina. She glared at him. "It used to be Anasazi pots though, wasn't it, Val?" he said.

Her green eyes kindled beneath the glow of his smile. Valentina looked him over contemptuously from flowing turban to patent leather shoes. On closer inspection the pink design in his tie turned out to be "Happy Faces."

"And you used to be a geologist, Harry. What happened? Flunk your comprehensives on igneous rocks?" she said haughtily.

Loretta stared from one to the other. They didn't appear to remember she was there. "You know each other?"

Harry's smile never dimmed, it just altered slightly in candlelight intensity. "Very well. Or at least we did once. We were at UNLV together."

Loretta looked at the furious glare on her granddaughter's face. It cheered her immensely. Valentina hadn't shown any emotion other than weary acceptance in a long time. "At the university in Las Vegas?" she echoed. "But I thought you were Hadi al-Bakil."

"I knew him as Harry Smith," Valentina grated out. "But it doesn't surprise me that he was using an alias. He told me he was from northeastern Nevada, up in Elko, not Arabia."

"I'm from both. It's a long story." Harry cleared his throat, his stance radiating a slight uneasiness. "I didn't lie to you, Val. I am from Elko. My stepfather has a nice little ranch up that way. Pete Smith." Harry turned to Loretta. "You'd like him, ma'am," he said, his voice giving the courtesy title just a slight Western drawl. "He votes Republican."

Valentina sighed in disgust. Of all the things Harry could possibly remember it had to be that her grandfather had been a Republican.

Loretta's grin was girlish with pleasure. "Pete Smith has my approval," she said. "What is your mother's name? Perhaps I know her. My late husband was a state senator from Nevada."

Harry grimaced slightly. "Ah, Bunny. Her name is Bunny Smith."

A faint smile curved Valentina's lips. She hadn't known he was embarrassed about his mother's given name.

Loretta shook her head sadly. "No, I don't think I know her. I'm sure I'd remember that name."

"People usually do," Harry agreed ruefully.

"But if you are from northern Nevada, how can you be from Arabia as well? And have two names?"

"An AKA," Valentina said. "Isn't that what the police call it? Also Known As."

Harry looked theatrically crushed. "Cruel, Val, really cruel. My dad is a Yemeni. Generally I only use his name when in Arabia, but the cultural exchange people thought Hadi al-Bakil had a nicer ring to it than Harry Smith. I don't think they wanted it known that I was born in Chicago."

"A blemish on our honor if it be known," a second man said. He stood quietly at Harry's back, a giant in full Bedouin dress including a curved scimitar and jewel-handled dagger. His black beard bristled. His brows were equally bushy. They sat low on his forehead creating a foliage-like screen for his deep-set eyes. His skin was the color of lovingly buffed mahogany.

Loretta's hands raised in nervous surprise. Her eyes widened in shock at the giant's derogatory statement.

Valentina looked interested. She rather liked the tone of the man's insult.

Harry's lips twitched. "Ladies, allow me to present my associate, interpreter, and, much to his chagrin, my friend, Ahmed."

The giant stared at each of the women in turn but said nothing more.

"I've mentioned Val Crosby before, I think. And this is her grandmother."

Ahmed's black eyes flickered over Loretta and dismissed her. They perused Valentina at length, causing her to blush furiously. The giant's smile was evil. He spoke only to Harry. "Her eyes are those of a gazelle. *Ma sha'Allah*, may Allah protect," he said, the deep sound of his voice rumbling in his broad chest.

"That is a compliment, Val," Harry said.

Valentina's eyes narrowed suspiciously but Loretta beamed at Ahmed with approval. "*Shukran*, Ahmed," she said. Then added, aside to her granddaughter, "That means 'thanks' in Arabic."

Ahmed rolled his eyes heavenward.

Harry laughed. "Finally got your comeuppance, you old phoney," he told the giant and caught the attention of a passing waiter. After verifying he'd caught the vintage tray rather than the Perrier one, a concession to the Muslim guests of honor, Harry passed each of the women a fresh glass of champagne. He took two for himself before letting the waiter continue on his round of the room. Ahmed ignored the tray and its alcoholic refreshments.

Harry raised the drink in his right hand. "To old friends and their charming relatives," he said. "*Fi sahad tak!*"

Loretta joined in his toast but had to jog Valentina's elbow before the young woman took a sip of her own champagne.

"And what does that mean?" Loretta inquired, as Harry finished off his first glass and thrust the empty goblet into Ahmed's huge hand. The Bedouin frowned at him but said nothing.

Harry grinned. "It translates loosely as 'To your health.' One of my few Arabic phrases. My ... er ... flirtation with learning the language has not withstood the years. I knew far more when I was a kid and spent part of each summer with my father. Compared to the rest of the Yemenis here, I'm fairly illiterate. Ahmed thinks I am a disgrace to the commission."

"Perhaps you are," Valentina said quietly.

The shocked look on her grandmother's face told her the remark had embarrassed Loretta. It had been better left unsaid. Valentina wondered why she had said it. Did her bitterness over the past run so deep that she felt she had lash out at Harry when he was only being sociable? He probably felt nothing for her anymore.

Valentina put her champagne glass aside and looked across the room as if responding to a signal from another guest. "Excuse me. There is someone I must talk to," she mumbled and moved away, her eyes not really seeing any one face in the crowd.

Harry let out a long, low sigh. "Damn," he muttered and quickly finished off his second glass. "I had a feeling I was going to need more than one drink."

"I don't know what got into her," Loretta apologized. "I'm appalled, Mr. Bakil. Please don't ..."

"Harry. I prefer Harry. And don't apologize. The hurt goes two ways. Did you ever wonder why I didn't come after her when she ran away from Vegas five years ago?"

Loretta looked after her granddaughter's back. Valentina had not stopped to talk to anyone although a few people had turned expectantly toward her. She had fled from the room without a backward look. "Frankly, no, I didn't, Harry." At his startled look, Loretta smiled. "You see, dear, I never knew you existed."

Chapter Two

HARRY DREW LORETTA off to the side of the room into an alcove where a scattering of aluminum-framed chairs did little to encourage a comfortable tête-à-tête. After seating the elderly woman in one, Harry pulled another chair up, facing her. He leaned forward, his elbows resting on his knees. The white silk of his open burnoose dragged on the floor. He had unbuttoned his suit jacket and now his tie with its grinning little pink faces swung gently back and forth as he moved. Ahmed stood like an armed honor guard at Harry's side, his arms crossed over his chest, his stance a military dress-ease. He looked the embodiment of an evil *jinn* newly released from captivity in a bottle.

"Let me get this straight," Harry said, his voice hushed. "Val never told you about me?"

Loretta met the worried expression in his blue eyes, her own green eyes sparkling with delight. Harry recognized those eyes. They were Valentina's eyes.

"Should she have?" Loretta asked.

His hand moved to run through his dark hair in a distracted reflex and bumped into the turban knocking it askew. He frowned slightly and plucked the headgear off, balancing it on his knee. Damn, he'd never get used to wearing the stupid thing. The commission was nuts to think they could turn an American geologist into an Arabian prince, despite his father's bloodlines. He belonged to the ranch in Nevada, not the mountain city in the Yemeni highlands.

"She never mentioned me at all?" he demanded, incredulous. "But we went together for a year and a half. Hell, we even..." He stopped short, realizing he'd almost said too much. If Loretta Crosby hadn't known her granddaughter had been seeing him, she sure as hell didn't want to discover he and Valentina had shared a bed.

Loretta's face creased in a smile of animated pleasure. Valentina would age as gracefully as her grandmother, Harry thought. They had the same lovely cheekbones, the same glowing skin. Loretta's years had treated her kindly, leaving only a scattering of wrinkles as an endowment of time. Most were smile lines that creased her cheeks and gathered in the corners of her eyes.

"You lived together!" Loretta breathed.

Harry looked apologetic, sheepish over his slip of the tongue.

"That's wonderful!" Loretta leaned forward and patted his hand. "There's hope for her yet." She looked intently into Harry's face. "Now I wonder why she never said a word about your existence?"

"I wanted to marry her," Harry offered, feeling he had to explain his own behavior. "I hadn't actually proposed though."

"That usually doesn't cause a girl to run away," Loretta said. "At least not from a man like you."

Harry hunched his broad shoulders uneasily.

"That's merely a personal observation, Harry," Loretta assured him. "If I were Val's age I'd do all in my power to get you to notice me."

Harry looked disconsolate. "That was one of the problems, Mrs. Crosby. Other women."

Loretta dismissed the idea with a wave of her hand. "Nonsense. You already told me you wanted to marry Val. If she was jealous that other women saw your worth ..."

He laughed. The word "worth" would not have occurred to the predatory women who had flaunted their availability, and their beds, at him over the years.

"All right," Loretta said. "Your charm, if you will." At his wide, wolfish grin, she chuckled. "Val's a fool, Harry." She paused, studying him. "How do you feel about her now?"

"Now?" He glanced across the room in the direction that Valentina had disappeared. "She's too damn thin, for one thing. She looks almost anorexic. And too smooth. The Val I knew was real. Her hair used to be pulled back in a long tail that hung down past her shoulders." It had swayed jauntily from side to side as she walked, he remembered. He had always enjoyed following Valentina, enjoyed watching her hips swing with each long, loping step she took. He had followed that enticing view around campus until she had noticed him.

"And Val never could keep her hair neat," Loretta agreed. "There were always strands that hung loose."

Lost temporarily in remembrance, Harry nodded. "Caramel-colored wisps about her face," he murmured. "I used to brush them back ..." Before kissing her and carrying her to bed, he thought, caught in the sweet memory.

"Excellent," Loretta announced. "You still love her."

Harry looked trapped momentarily. Then he squared his shoulders and sat back in his chair. "What good is that though, Mrs. Crosby? I'm not blind. I saw that Val's wearing an engagement ring. A bigger rock than I'd ever be able to give her. Despite the hoopla of this thing," he waved a hand to indicate the cultured murmur of the reception. "I'm nothing but a soon-to-be unemployed geologist. My contact with the Marib archaeological unit is up soon. I have nothing to offer Val."

"You love her."

"So does her fiancé."

Loretta gave a ladylike snort. "He is squashing Val's real personality. She is being molded to fit Todd's specifications."

"And she's letting him?" Harry demanded in astonishment. The Valentina he had known had fought tooth and nail to get her own way. "She's changed."

"Do you know why?" Loretta persisted.

"Me." He said it in a monotone. "What I did, or rather what she thought I did. It was all a misunderstanding but we were both too damn proud to talk it out." His eyes reflected the pain of Valentina's sudden disappearance, and his own stubborn refusal to follow her. How often over the past five years had he regretted the whole farce? How often had he wanted to turn back the clock, to win Valentina's love once more? Too often, Harry admitted to himself. Since then he had looked for some part of Valentina in every woman he met. But Valentina Crosby had been elusive, her quirks too individual and endearing to be found in another woman's face.

Harry leaned forward and impulsively covered Loretta's hands with his own. "I'd win her back if I could," he said. "But I don't think Val would give me the chance, Mrs. Crosby."

Loretta grinned back at his serious face. "That's all I wanted to hear," she declared softly and squeezed his hands. "And, please, call me Loretta, dear. You and I have got a lot of talking to do."

Valentina balked when Loretta confronted her an hour later. "What do you mean I owe it to him? I have no intention of seeing Harry Smith alone."

"You won't be alone. Ahmed will be there." Loretta smiled. "Actually I think he's rather dear, don't you?"

"Harry?"

"Ahmed, dear. He acts more like a bodyguard than an associate."

Valentina stopped a waiter and helped herself to a glass of champagne. She knew she'd had far too many glasses already but she also knew her grandmother. There would be no getting around a showdown with Harry.

Loretta pushed Valentina toward the patio. Because of the threat of rain, the outdoor area had been closed to the reception guests. It had taken Loretta only a moment to obtain the key—a lifetime in Washington politics had its compensations. It only took a dropped name or an arch look and somebody's closet rattled with the bones of an old scandal. In this case though, the man with the key had been in love with Loretta for years. It made her feel young again to have him so eager to do as she requested.

"And I don't think you owe it to Harry to see him," Loretta informed her granddaughter smugly. "You owe it to me because you kept him a secret. I'm ashamed of you, Val. Why he was practically part of the family."

Valentina flushed. "Grandma! I ..."

"I like him," Loretta said. Her tone accepted no rebuttals. "You owe him an apology for your lack of manners earlier, if nothing else, Val."

"But ..."

They had reached the patio door. Through the open slats of the vertical blinds Loretta recognized Ahmed's broad back. Loretta was glad she had given Harry the key before looking for her grand-daughter. She doubted she would have been able to keep Valentina prisoner long without help.

Loretta opened the door and gave her granddaughter a slight push of encouragement. "Go on. I'll be right here waiting for you."

"You mean you'll be here to make sure I don't cut and run," Valentina said.

"It's fortunate that I know you so well, dear." Loretta gave her a quick smile and shut the door in Valentina's face. From the other side of the glass door she made shoo-ing gestures at her young relative, then pulled the blind closed.

Reluctant, Valentina moved past Ahmed's motionless form, and turned to face Harry.

He stood at the far side of the patio area, his back to the view of city lights. A wall surrounded the flagged terrace. Overhead a lattice-work roof had been built. In later years ivy would cover it but now only new shoots were entwined around the base of the supports. A few pots filled with green plants hung from the overhead beams. The soft night breeze pushed them so that they swung gently to and fro. There were a number of cement benches in the area. They were arranged to give visitors varied glimpses of the city skyline. Valentina chose one and sat down, her legs crossed. One foot twitched impatiently. She looked across to where Harry leaned back against the wall.

He was staring up at the night sky, at the patterns the spotlights created against the clouds. "You once told me that when you were a little girl you thought the searchlights were looking for babies tied to stars. Remember, Val?" he asked softly.

She was touched that he recalled the foolish childhood fantasy. She twisted the now empty champagne glass, rocking the crystal stem back and forth between her fingers. "There are no stars tonight, Harry."

He turned away from the night sky. "And how about in your life, Val. Are there stars there? Are you happy?"

"Of course I am. Ecstatic. Don't I look it?"

More important, Harry thought, she didn't sound ecstatic. He watched her foot in its ridiculously high heeled sandal swing back and forth. Did she remember how long shapely legs in black stockings affected him? Valentina's legs had always been very long and very shapely. The split skirt of her black dress had fallen open to display a generous amount of thigh as well. As if she became aware of it only when his gaze lingered, Valentina uncrossed her legs and pulled her skirt back together.

"Actually, Val, you look like hell," Harry said.

Her lips twitched slightly. She had expected a smooth compliment but was glad she hadn't received one. She'd always expected something different from Harry. He'd never been like other men she met. Perhaps that was why she was having such a hard time forgetting him.

"I can't say much for you either, Harry. That beard makes you look like a bit player in an amateur production of *Kismet*." All the same, the temptation to run her finger over that jaw-rimming dark beard was nearly overpowering.

He ran a hand along the close-clipped growth, a cocky smile in his eyes. "You don't like it?"

She wouldn't agree to that. Instead she shifted her gaze to the white folds of fabric wound around his head. "The turban has got to go."

He was grinning at her now. Valentina wished he wouldn't.

She stared down at the thin-stemmed wine glass in her hand. Her heart cried for him, for the anguished sweetness of a love that had been perfect. Or she had thought it perfect. Had wanted it to be perfect.

Harry looked down at her bowed head, at the way her new, shorter hairdo fell forward, the lovely brown tresses hiding her expression. She was so cosmopolitan now, a product of the city. Was the sophisticated black dress with its padded shoulders, draped sleeves and dipping neckline a front or had the girl who'd once owned nothing but faded jeans really disappeared? He took advantage of her preoccupation to search for a clue in her appearance, and was relieved to find one. Valentina still had her nervous habit. Her nails were gently curved, of a moderate length, and coated with a clear polish. But the tip of one nail showed definite signs of having been bitten recently. Because it reminded him of the girl he'd loved, Harry thought the ragged nail was beautiful.

He watched the revolutions of the empty goblet in Valentina's hand. He fought the urge to go to her, to take her in his arms once more. Harry waited for a sign. Prayed for a signal that she wasn't as immune to him as she appeared.

Valentina abandoned the champagne glass, setting it aside on the bench. She looked up into his face. "So, Harry," she said. Her voice was that of a disinterested but polite guest. "Tell me how a geologist came to be part of an archaeological team."

The timing was wrong after all. The prayer unanswered. Harry was glad he hadn't rushed his fences. "That's easily explained, Val. I'm their petrography expert."

If her tone had been apathetic, at least Valentina's blank expression was sincere, he noted with relief.

"Petrography? You were working with it at school, weren't you," she said. "Looking at rock fragments through a microscope."

"Through a polarizing microscope," he corrected. "And the fragments were thin slices of material. Back then I identified fine-grained minerals in rocks. The microscope made otherwise invisible textures visible for classification."

Valentina nodded. "I remember. You were quite good at it."

Harry took the statement at face value. She had merely been stating a fact from the past. He moved closer to her bench, leaning a shoulder against one of the porch supports.

"How is it used in archaeology though?" she asked.

The breeze stirred her hair. It was still the color of dark caramel candy but some of the luster was missing. He recalled all too well how it looked with the early morning sun seeking out the scattering of natural, paler highlights. He remembered the soft feel of it beneath his hands, beneath his cheek on a pillow.

Valentina pushed back a lock as it blew across her mouth. She was very aware that Harry's eyes followed her movement and lingered on her lips.

"I was studying potsherds," he said. "There are a number of different ways to use geology in identifying artifacts. But in this case I was supposed to look for rock types in the clay makeup of sherds from various localities."

Something stirred in her eyes, a faint but still well-remembered glow. Valentina's face turned up to his in fascination. Harry took one step further. He sat on the end of the bench and tested the word that had once been life, passion and magic to her. Pottery.

Valentina hardly noticed. The old thrill she had fought when looking at the artifacts in the cases had come back. This time it was stronger. Was it because she was with Harry or because he was talking about the only other love she had forsaken ... her fascination with the pottery of ancient peoples?

"The objective was to note features that would make the pieces from one dig site distinctive from those of another," Harry continued. "My job was to ID dust-sized rock particles in the composition using cross sections of the pottery."

His voice washed over her as he went into more detail. She heard the familier words—schist, clay, quartz, feldspar, shale—as if in a dream. They conjured up visions, not of rock types, but of glorious days spent together in the desert sun. Weekends of shared laughter and love.

In those happier days, Harry had enjoyed introducing her to the finer elements of his field. He had led her from one mountain range to another in the Las Vegas valley. The tilted formations of the Spring Mountains, the rose-tinted granite around Frenchman's Mountain. Valentina knew them all. But it hadn't been geologic layers she had seen. It had been the love of his subject that shone in Harry's eyes. Eyes that even now were as clear and guileless as the western sky.

Valentina tried to push the memories away but they were too strong and in the end she resisted no longer. Instead her mind wandered to one particularly poignant day. The day Harry had taken her to see the fossils.

She had always considered fossils to be impressions in the rock. Those were the kind she'd found on hikes with the Girl Scouts in junior high school and in the museums she visited. Just the imprinted skeleton forms of extinct forms of life. But Harry's discovery hadn't looked dead and forgotten. His fossils had looked alive and vibrant.

He had never told her if the delicate sea shells were his find, his secret, or merely one of the wonders of the valley encountered on the geology class field trips. They had been as pink and perfect as if they had been freshly washed by the sea. The tiny fossils had looked like miniatures of the curled conch shells that lined the shelves in oceanside souvenir shops. She wondered if it was possible to hear the sound of the ancient sea in their tightly rolled centers. It seemed impossible to believe they were remnants from another era, an eon not viewed by man. Stranded on the beaches of a forgotten sea when the climate changed, the shells had metamorphosed into a substance harder than the sands in which they rested.

When she'd reached for them, her touch both fearful and awed, Harry's hand had joined hers, guiding, teaching her the wonders of nature through her sensitive fingertips. Through him she had also learned to see the beauty in the crumbling red sandstone arches of the Valley of Fire. Had revelled in the sparkling mirror-like finish found in paper thin flakes of mica and in the towering, multi-sided crystal structures of amethyst in shades from palest lavender to deepest royal purple. They had found both in their rambles.

Archaeology had been her religion, but once upon a time Harry had turned the mysteries of geology into poetry for her.

Valentina's eyes sparkled with a hint of unshed tears. They had been beautiful days. What had gone wrong? Had she been too wrapped up in her own studies, too blind to see him slipping away from her?

"Harry, I ..." Her voice was a harsh whisper, as if the tightness in her throat held the words back.

Her eyes shone as brightly as diamonds, as lovely as moonbeams on a crystal sea. He read pain and hurt in their watery depths. Harry leaned toward her wanting to ease her suffering. "Val," he murmured.

His tone was low, intimate. She remembered the chill of anticipation she'd always felt when he said her name with that hint of wonder in his voice. Valentina felt it again, and bent toward him. "Harry," she whispered.

"It's been a long time, honey," he said.

"Too long."

Their lips were a breath apart when there was a sharp sound, similar to that of a car backfire. Then the clay pot that swung just behind them exploded.

Valentina jerked in surprise then found herself pulled to the ground as Ahmed shouted a sharp gutteral command and charged onto the patio. She lay there a moment, her cheek pressed to the cool, smooth flagstone. She could feel the hard, lean, remembered length of Harry's body covering hers. His tie with its ludicrous collection of grinning faces was flipped back over his shoulder. The short, thick bristles of his beard scraped against her cheek. His scent surrounded her in a combination of exotic cologne and tart champagne. Intoxicating—if she let if be. But the jolt as she'd hit the hardness of the stone flooring had made her realize just how close she had come to throwing away her future with Todd, how close she had come to succumbing to Harry once more.

"What the hell do you think you are doing?" she growled and tried to push him away.

Harry had lost his turban. His hair was the same blend of soft brown and raven's wing black she remembered from of old. It fell forward over his brow in disarray. His eyes were no longer gentle as they had been a moment before. They looked scared. "Damn it, Val," he hissed. "Keep down. Someone's shooting at us."

"As in guns and bullets?"

"It sure as hell isn't guns and roses, honey." She hadn't changed her brand of perfume. The thought passed fleetingly through his mind, totally irrelevant to the way his heart was pounding. His breath came in gasps. He'd longed for her so long and he could so easily have lost her to a sniper's bullet. Harry tightened his grip about Valentina's shoulders holding her close.

Valentina forced herself to ignore the fearful pounding of Harry's heart so near her ear. She raised her head an inch to stare at the towering form of Ahmed. He had unsheathed his scimitar and stood in the middle of the patio waving it in a threatening manner at his unseen enemy.

"Good God! Hasn't he seen *Raiders of the Lost Ark?*" Valentina cried. "Somebody's gonna shoot him!"

No further shots were forthcoming. Instead a small army of security men tumbled through the patio door. Ahmed glared at them, then slid his curved saber back into its sheath.

"*Kif halak?*" he rumbled.

Harry gave the man a quick nod of relief. His hold on Valentina eased slightly. It was hard to release her when his mind and body both urged him never to let her go. "Okay. We're okay. *Mabsut, ilhamdulillah*," Harry mumbled in response to Ahmed's calm inquiry. He rolled off Valentina's now squirming form, and sat upright. "Fine, thanks be to Allah."

Ahmed nodded and returned to his place near the door, apparently content that no harm had occurred.

Valentina accepted the help of a uniformed security guard in getting to her feet. Two others buttonholed Harry, firing rapid questions at him. There were armed men everywhere but they did little to make her feel safe. What kind of crackpot took potshots at a museum building? Someone who nursed an extreme hatred toward Arabs? It seemed to be the only explanation.

To cover the fact that she was shaking, Valentina bent to retrieve Harry's turban before letting the guard escort her back into the building. Then she froze.

"Harry."

He turned away from the security guards and their questions. There was a note of fear in Valentina's voice that he had never heard before.

"Harry," she whispered once more. Her eyes were wide and nearly blank when they met his across the few feet that separated them. Her face had turned a ghastly white. "Look," she said.

She turned the tightly-rolled turban in her hands. One pink fingertip peeked at him from the crown then withdrew leaving the hole in the turban exposed. A very neat bullet hole.

Chapter Three

ONLY A FEW clouds played in the sky over Washington the next day. They looked like puffy cotton balls. Through the tinted glass of his windshield, Harry identified them from habit: fair weather clouds. He climbed out of the rented Oldsmobile and slammed the driver's door. The highly-buffed surface of the hood reflected the pattern in the sky but in shades of diplomat silver-gray. Fair weather. He hoped like hell they forecast more than just the climate. He needed all the help he could get.

He paused, waiting for Ahmed to maneuver his broad frame from the passenger seat. Harry surveyed the neat yard and two-story red brick house as if he expected it to be ringed with a collection of fiendish traps. A short hedge encircled the property. The lawn was manicured, an even deep green. Roses climbed a trellis, shielding the front porch. Flowers bloomed in sculptured beds, their fragile petals tinted in every color of the spectrum.

The sweet edge of suburbia. It might as well have been the realm of a fearsome *efreet*. Harry took a deep breath, collecting his courage before attempting to walk up the cement path to the door.

At the house, the edge of a curtain in an upstairs room twitched. The radiant face and white hair of his fellow conspirator appeared briefly. She motioned to him, pointing down at the main door.

Harry took a deep breath and took the plunge. No *jinns*, no *efreets*, threatened his approach along the walkway. But then he knew the pit yawned inside the house rather than outside.

Valentina didn't know he was expected.

He leaned on the doorbell. It played a few bars of a song. He found it naggingly familiar, something classical, but he was too tense to identify it. The sound of a vacuum cleaner droned in the house. As the last strains of the chimes faded away, the vacuum died with a sigh. Harry held his breath.

In the front room, Valentina wearily pushed a straggling lock of hair back from her face, trying to hook it behind her ear. It was too short and swung back to lay in its accustomed place just under her chin. She brushed at it in irritation and pulled the door open.

Time rolled away for her. This was the Harry Smith she knew so well. The trappings of Arabia were nearly gone now, as was the quiet, dignified suit and whimsical tie. His dark hair waved out of control, tumbling about his ears and along the nape of his neck. He had brushed it back from his brow, but even there the waves inched forward. He still wore the devastatingly close-cut beard. It looked even more intriguing in daylight. His shirt was white with a thin blue stripe. The collar and two buttons were open to display a sun-browned, broad section of his chest. The cuffs of his long sleeves were rolled under just once so that the fabric skimmed his wrists. His jeans were well worn, faded, and tight. They hugged his narrow hips and clung to his thighs. His Nike running shoes were scuffed and hadn't been white in a long time.

What really sent Valentina's heart skipping was the sight of his sunglasses. Harry's trademark, she thought. Mirrored lenses. They reflected her own face in duplicate. She had always hated those shades. She still did. But seeing them once more was endearing. Harry hadn't changed at all. She wondered if that was good or bad.

"What are you doing here?" she challenged, afraid he would hear the catch in her voice.

Her hair was pulled back. Unsuccessfully so. It straggled from haphazardly placed bobby pins. The sight made him want to smooth the wisps back, to comb his fingers through the golden brown wealth. To kiss her.

As if she read the thought in his face, Valentina stepped back into the room and held the door wide. "I suppose Grandma invited you," she said.

Harry grinned and removed his sunglasses, sticking them in his shirt pocket. They dangled out, suspended by one ear piece.

Valentina looked wonderful, he thought. She was once again the girl with whom he'd fallen in love. From her flying hair to her pale jeans, T-shirt and sneakers, she was beautiful. Her shirt was oversized, baggy, and advertised the Washington Redskins. Her shoes were pink high tops with matching laces. Her jeans had a chic tear in the knee and hung loosely on her slim form. That meant her loss of weight was of recent origin, Harry decided.

"As it happens, yes, Loretta did invite me," he said and stepped inside. A silent Ahmed followed him. "She said something about lunch."

The interior décor was as well groomed as the outside of the house. The flowered Wedgwood-blue upholstery on the long sofa and comfortable side chairs matched. It was accented by solid color drapes in a deeper blue, pale blue walls, and plush wall-to-wall carpeting in a dusky blue-gray shade. The end tables were a deep cherry and highly buffed. The lemony scent of Pledge hung heavy in the air. Off-white beanpot styled lamps with pleated linen shades sat like bookends on the tables at each end of the sofa.

It was the wall behind the couch that caught and held Harry's interest though. It was a collage of photographs, some in black and white, some in fading color. There were all of Valentina. Valentina at four astride a pony. Valentina at seven, a tiny, delicate ballerina. The wall charted her life from skinned knees and roller skates to prom dress and diploma.

Valentina shut the front door and returned to the waiting upright vacuum where it sat in the center of the room. She gave the long cord a vicious yank, taking out her frustration on it. It pulled the plug neatly out of the wall socket. A second tug resulted in the sweeper sucking up its cord like a long strand of spaghetti.

Would her grandmother ever give up? For weeks Loretta had dropped hints about Todd's lack of desirability as an in-law. Now she had brought Harry into the battle. Well, it wasn't going to work, Valentina told herself. Harry Smith was a part of the past. Long over and nearly forgotten. Nearly.

"Lunch!" Valentina muttered in disgust and thrust the vacuum into a hall closet. "Well I hope you finally acquired a taste for peanut butter. 'Cause on Saturday, that's all we've got."

Harry was right behind her as Valentina led the way into the kitchen. It was color-coordinated with appliances and cupboards of fire-engine red. Bright geraniums bloomed in a box outside the window. Their color was repeated in the large red and white plaid design of both the wallpaper and the dish towels.

"Peanut butter? I was hoping for something better," Harry said. "Steak, perhaps."

Valentina busied herself in the pantry. Steak. Just the thought of it made her mouth water. But Todd was adamant on the new diet. Red meat was a killer, he claimed. Vegetables, fish and poultry were the only items allowed on the menu. After six months, she was sick to death of poultry, fish and vegetables. Especially since, on principle, she hated all types of fish, and wasn't keen about broccoli, cauliflower, or brussels sprouts—all Todd's favorite foods.

Harry pulled out a kitchen chair and leaned back in it, making himself at home. Valentina plunked a loaf of uncracked wheat bread in front of him and a jar of Peter Pan chunky-style peanut butter. Harry stared at the package of bread in dislike, his dark brows drawing together over the bridge of his hawkish nose. Valentina didn't blame him. She would willingly have killed for a thick, soft slice of white bread. Poison to the system but, oh, so good.

"How about if Ahmed and I take you and Loretta out for lunch?" Harry suggested.

Valentina dropped into a chair across from him and pushed the lank lock of hair back again. "Why not just leave me out of it, Harry."

"Nonsense, Val," Loretta declared. She squeezed past the bulky form of Ahmed in the doorway. He eyed her lavender pant suit with disgust. Unabashed, Loretta twinkled up at the giant. "Good afternoon, Ahmed. How are you today?"

Ahmed stood in his accustomed stance, arms folded, legs spread. His *djellaba* was striped in rust and blue. His turban was a deeper shade of copper. A long swatch of it was draped from his left ear across his chest and tossed negligently over his right shoulder. It made him look arrogant. Although he had abandoned his scimitar, the sheaf of his *jambiya* was thrust into his broad, embroidered belt. "*Es-salaam aleikum, jadda aat,*" was the big man's rough greeting.

Loretta's smile grew wider in delight. She looked to Harry for a translation.

"May peace be with you, grandmother," he interpreted.

"Peace is a lovely word," Loretta said and looked up at the stern dark face of the giant. "I would share it with you, Ahmed."

"*Wa aleikum es salaam*," Harry said. "And on you be peace."

Loretta turned to him eagerly. "Oh, yes, that sounds perfect, dear. Repeat it for me."

He did so, helping her through the syllables. When she had stumbled through the final word, Loretta took the chair Harry held for her and beamed around at the three young people. Ahmed's face was still closed and inscrutable. Harry's was leery. Valentina scowled at her grandmother.

"Well, children." Loretta folded her hands together on the table. "No ill effects after our excitement last night?" she asked. "Did the police find anything? Oh, Val. Not peanut butter. It tastes dreadful on that bread from the health food store. Besides, I feel more like Chinese."

"I vote for Chinese, too," Harry said reclaiming his own chair. "Mounds of fluffy white rice topped with sweet and sour pork."

Ahmed made a strangled sound.

"You don't have to eat it," Harry assured him and turned back to the ladies. "Pork is taboo in the Islamic world. I've been starved for the taste of it. The Arabs have some delicious food, but after a year of nothing else my enthusiasm for it paled."

He picked up the jar of peanut butter and held it loosely, staring unseeing at the ingredients written on the label. "The police did find something, but it wasn't much help. The sniper's rifle was in the parking lot. Under the chief of security's car. No fingerprints."

Loretta sighed. "No leads at all?"

Harry grinned at her and set the jar aside. "Not that they told me about, at least."

"So we'll never know why we were shot at," Valentina said. "Just some nut on a shooting spree who thought we were an easy target."

Harry's eyes were serious. "No, I think it was deliberate, Val," he said.

"Deliberate! You mean somebody wants to kill you?"

"Or scare me."

"Why ever do you say that?" Loretta demanded, intrigued. "Have there been other attempts?"

He nodded. "But not on me. When we got back to the hotel last night there was a message from my cousin's wife. It seems that Badr was attacked two days ago."

Two days. It still bothered him that Sikina had waited so long to notify him. Not that he could do anything for Badr. But the time delay was curious. Sikina's message hadn't told Harry much and he had been unable to reach her either at Badr's home or at the hospital. All he knew from his transatlantic call earlier in the day was that Badr was in a stable condition.

"My God," Valentina breathed. "Is he all right?"

"He's alive. Other than that, I'm in the dark. The hospital wouldn't release any information."

Loretta's face was pale beneath a light application of blusher. Her hand touched Harry's on the table. "Oh, my dear, I am so sorry. You think there is a connection?"

Harry shrugged. "I don't know. I could just be jumping at shadows."

"What's your cousin do?" Valentina asked. Her brow creased in thought. "I mean, it isn't anything illegal, is it?"

"Depends on your point of view," Harry said. "Some people say Badr's a grave robber. Actually he's an archaeologist. Has an impressive track record with deciphering written records. Stuff that dates Before Christ."

"People don't usually shoot at archaeologists outside of those Indiana Jones movies," Loretta commented. "At least I didn't think they did."

"Badr was stabbed."

"Oh, dear."

Valentina leaned forward in her chair. "But what's the connection, Harry? That you're related? Do they have blood feuds in ... in ... where was it you were, anyway?"

"Yemen—It's south of Saudi Arabia—In the city of San'a'. It was my home base when I worked for the Marib excavation team."

For a moment Harry thought about the city and the sterile laboratory where he'd worked, bent over the microscope, analyzing mineral particles in pottery pieces. They had been fascinating hours, but of a temporary nature. His contract had been for a year, a deal finagled by his father, Dawud, and cousin, Badr. Dawud was content in his museum in Cairo and had surrendered the tall old house in San'a' to his only son with pleasure. The thick stone walls and heavily latticed windows had hidden a veritable paradise, a lush garden oasis. Flowers had been plentiful, especially the lovely Roses of at-Ta'if. Their scent had hung heavy in the air. A fountain had played day and night, its lyrical trickle at times soothing, at times irritating. It had been pleasant, luxurious, but it hadn't been home.

Harry looked across the table at Valentina. His gaze lingered on her high, prominent cheekbones, on the curve of her cheek, on the fullness of her lips. No, San'a' had never been home. Home was where Valentina Crosby was. She was home to him.

"I never heard of a blood feud," Harry said. "Badr and I are distant cousins, from two different tribal families. The Hashid and the Bakil were among the rulers of ancient San'a' in the twelfth century, but we've come down a notch or two in the last eight hundred years. Badr and I are more closely related through his wife Sikina, my second cousin."

Valentina turned her attention to the silent Ahmed. "Is there some family that would wish revenge on the Hashid *and* Bakil?" she asked.

The big man didn't move from his stance in the doorway. "There have been some misunderstandings," he rumbled.

"Great," Harry groaned. "I think we can take that as a definite maybe."

Valentina sighed. "So what comes next? A call to the Yemeni authorities?"

Harry pushed away from the table. "Lunch comes next. What's your favorite Chinese restaurant?"

Valentina's eyes narrowed. "How can you eat at a time like this? Your cousin is ..."

"He's okay. And I'm hungry."

"But ..."

"Val, he's safe in the hospital. From what I did learn, he could just as easily be dead. The attacker left him in the marketplace. It was hours till he was found. In all that time, don't you think whoever stabbed him could easily have come back and finished him off?"

She subsided in her chair. "But what about the shots last night?"

Harry further infuriated her by grinning. "They missed. Possibly on purpose. I don't think they meant to kill me. It was a warning."

A warning, Valentina thought. The memory of the bullet hole in the crown of his turban was still very fresh. If the sniper had "warned" them any closer, Harry Smith, alias Hadi al-Bakil, would be dead.

Loretta stood up and gave her jacket a tug to straighten it. "Lunch is definitely in order. We'll all think better on a full stomach. Do go change, Val. They have these wonderful luncheon specials at Ah Tuk's. If you hurry, we'll get there before the menu changes for evening."

Valentina opened her mouth to remind her grandmother that she had no intention of going out to lunch, then changed her mind. Maybe they could figure out what was going on. If she learned more about Badr's work, she might discover a piece of the mystery that Harry had overlooked. Harry might be brilliant in his own field, but that field was geology. She had always considered him to be highly intelligent. Just irresponsible. He was too closely involved to be able to sit back and look at the facts coolly. She, on the other hand, was detached from it all. Although she had put all interest in archaeology behind her, Valentina decided it wouldn't hurt to learn about the work at the Marib site. There might be a clue. Besides, she reasoned, Harry hadn't been alone when the shots were fired. *She* had been shot at as well.

"Give me five minutes," Valentina said and dashed up the stairs.

"Let's give her ten," Loretta suggested. She smiled at Harry. "I think she's weakening, dear."

He gave her a look filled with disbelief. "You're dreaming, Loretta. She still hates me."

"Oh, no, dear. Dislike, maybe, but not hate. After all, hate is the reverse of love and Val wouldn't want to admit to such strong emotions. She's cultivated the art of compromise the last few years. As long as she doesn't get too involved with anyone, she thinks she's safe."

"What about this Todd? She's engaged to him."

Loretta spoke thoughtfully. "Todd McAllister is safe, Harry. Boring, pompous, but definitely safe." She got to her feet as the door chimes struck their tune once more. "Trust me, Harry. Val will come to her senses. There's a certain look in her eyes when you're in the room. It gives me hope. Would you get the door for me? It's probably the paper boy. I'll get my purse."

Harry's chair scraped back. He didn't trust Loretta's intuition where her granddaughter was concerned. All he saw in Valentina's eyes was pain. Todd McAllister would probably make Valentina happy. Harry wasn't sure whether, given a second chance, he could be equally successful.

The best he could do was stick around and pray, he thought, and pulled open the front door.

It wasn't the newspaper boy. Even with the rising crime rate, young entrepreneurs didn't stick a gun in a customer's face.

The man behind the gun grinned at Harry's blank expression. His complexion was swarthy. His dark suit was ill-fitting. He looked unnatural without his *gitra* and burnoose. "*Salaam, Hadi ibn Dawud,*" he greeted.

Harry's heart dropped to the pit of his stomach. He backed into the room, his arms raised above his head. "*Marhaba.* Hi."

Behind the gunman, a second Yemeni laughed. "*Hayyaak alla.*" He chanted the traditional reply, his tone clearly sarcastic.

"A lovely thought," Harry agreed. "It's a shame I can't request Allah to preserve your life as well."

The man with the gun pushed into the house and snapped an order at his companion. The waving weapon forced Harry back, until he came up against the back of a flower printed armchair. Loretta stood posed in the kitchen doorway, her purse dangling from nerveless fingers. Her hand fluttered toward her chest. In the middle of the room, Ahmed stood like a statue. His dark eyes hardened. His only movement was to uncross his arms.

The gunman growled an order at his partner. The second man closed the door and leaned back against it. He fingered the handle of the jeweled *jambiya* stuck into the belt of his trousers.

"If you've come to kill me, I would prefer to leave the American woman's home," Harry said.

"*Efendi,* do not insult me," the gunman purred softly. His grin widened. Harry had an excellent view of very long incisors. "He who does not know the falcon will roast it," the man said.

Harry looked at the gun. "I feel more like a cooked goose with that pointed at me."

"You have but to tell us where the treasure rests," the gunman explained.

"And you will leave?" Harry glanced to the man with the dagger. "Even the *qayn*?" he asked in disbelief.

The idiot grin on the second man's face vanished at the insult. His dark eyes burned with hatred. The Bakil were *sharaf*, nobility. To have a mongrel member of the *sharaf* identify him as a man of low status and non-Arab descent enraged the Yemeni assassin.

The gunman shrugged, unconcerned that his partner had stiffened in anger. "The treasure," he repeated quietly. "It is of no use to you, *efendi*."

Harry tried to gauge the chances. One man had a gun, its deadly muzzle trained steadily on his own chest. The fact that the gunman considered him necessary was only a temporary and fleeting solace. The man would kill him with the same lack of concern with which he would swat a fly. It puzzled Harry that the Yemeni thought he knew the location of a treasure. What treasure?

"But a treasure is always of use," Harry said, his voice as steady and smooth as the gunman's. "Does not the wise one hold onto his crazy man in case a crazier one comes along? Or as we say in the States, a bird in the hand is worth two in the bush."

The gunman grew impatient. His smile faded. "Crazy men and birds are of little use, *efendi*. The treasure. Where is it hidden?"

Harry glanced aside at Ahmed. The giant hadn't moved, but his eyes were alert. Beyond him, Loretta's face had grown paler. She met his look, her own, one of terror. Harry felt a fresh surge of fear himself. Like Loretta, he had just caught the sound of a furtive step on the stairs. Valentina was carefully inching her way down from the second floor.

Adrenaline pumped through Harry's body. The Valentina he remembered had been renowned for her ability to act first and think second. Had she changed in that aspect? Loretta claimed that her granddaughter valued safety above all other virtues now. But did Valentina have a shred of common sense to keep her safe? Harry doubted it.

To get the full attention of the two assassins, Harry lowered his arms and leaned back against the chair. "Perhaps we could share. Half for you, half for me. There is more than enough to go around, enough to buy a dozen wives or more."

"Alas, I am a man cursed with greed," the gunman said. "I will take it all."

"But it must be sold to profit by it. I have the connections," Harry argued.

The gunman's smile returned, as distasteful and smug as before. "I also, *efendi*."

"A marketplace thief? You will not profit by him."

"You delay, Hadi son of Dawud."

"And you are foolish."

"*Yamkin.* Probably." The man raised the gun. "But you, *efendi*, will be dead."

It was the wrong thing to say.

Harry heard the sharp catch of Valentina's breath before she barrelled down the stairs, a gun in her hand.

The *qayn* at the door reacted a moment too late. His dagger sailed across the room and sank into the wall a full six inches shy of Valentina's crouched form.

The gunman's weapon exploded, then fell from his hand. His knees weakened. He sank to the floor, his fingers quivering a moment as he clutched at the jeweled hilt in his chest.

Ahmed's *jambiya* had not missed its target.

Valentina stared at the dead man. A few feet away, Harry was stretched full length on the carpet. As she watched, he leapt to his feet and lunged for the second Yemeni. The man's feet possessed a fleetness his dagger had lacked. He was out the door and into the waiting car before Harry reached the middle of the front yard.

Her mind in a haze of disbelief, Valentina watched the assassin escape. It had all happened so fast.

Harry lunged back through the open door. His blue eyes blazed. Anger, fear, and frustration flickered in quick succession over his face.

"Who the hell do you think you are?" he thundered crossing the room quickly to tower over Valentina. "Rambo?"

He pried the gun from Valentina's now nerveless fingers. It was heavy, long barrelled. An antique. It belonged on the hip of a gunslinger in a Roy Rogers western.

"Jesus, Val! What were you going to do with this thing? Challenge them to a showdown on Main Street?"

His verbal attack kept Valentina's attention centered on him, not on the body of the dead gunman. Harry was relieved when Valentina's chin came up in a gesture of defense.

"I took it from Grandpa's collection," she said, her voice cold with anger. "It wasn't loaded."

At Valentina's admission, Loretta gave a horrified gasp and slid gracefully toward the floor in a faint. Harry caught her in his arms.

Valentina grasped one of her grandmother's pale hands. The veins seemed more prominent, the skin parchment thin. Her green eyes met Harry's, anguished and newly frightened. "Oh, God," she breathed.

"She's just fainted, honey," he said. "She'll be all right."

Twenty-four hours before, Harry Smith had been just a memory she had wished she could forget. Now he knelt on one knee in the kitchen doorway, the unconscious form of her grandmother gently cradled in his arms. His tenderness stirred something in Valentina's soul. She couldn't imagine Todd in the same protective stance. It didn't matter that she couldn't imagine Todd ever putting either her grandmother or herself in a life-threatening situation as Harry had done even though he hadn't meant to.

Over Loretta's head, he glared at Valentina, then at the ornate hilt of the dagger in the wall. "You could have been killed, Val," he said quietly.

The pain in his voice sent a chill of fear racing up Valentina's spine. She hadn't considered the consequences; hadn't realized how close she had come to death. Somehow things had become so confused, so natural. When she had heard the assassin calmly announce Harry's imminent death, something had snapped inside her. It hadn't been a conscious decision that drove her down the stairs and into the living room. It had been fear. Fear for Harry Smith, a man she professed to hate.

Valentina stared at the *jambiya*. The knife blade was hidden within the plaster. To fight the choking sensation of fear in her throat, Valentina turned away from the dagger only to notice the corpse in the center of the living room rug. Terror rose from the pit of her stomach, widening her eyes, making her breathing short and sharp. It could just as easily have been her form lying there waiting for the coroner.

Valentina glanced once more at the *jambiya* so close to her side and swallowed quickly. "Harry, I ..."

But he had already turned away from her. He swept Loretta up and carried her into the kichen, away from the carnage. "Call an ambulance," he ordered over his shoulder. "And the police."

Valentina watched helplessly as Harry eased his fragile burden into a chair by the table. In quick order he had found a bottle of Pine Sol and waved the odoriferous fumes under her grandmother's nose.

"I already called the police," Valentina said, her voice sullen. "From the upstairs phone. They should be here any minute." Telephoning for the ambulance would get her out of the room, though. Away from the dead man in the living room and the sight of her reviving grandmother. She felt so helpless. Placing the call would at last keep her occupied and push her terror and guilt away, if only temporarily.

Valentina started to turn away and then stopped, frozen in her tracks.

Harry heard her sharp intake of breath and glared over his shoulder at her. "The paramedics, Val," he urged.

She didn't move. "Ahmed," she said, her voice a mere whisper.

Harry turned quickly. He crossed the room in two strides.

Ahmed stood over the dead gunman's body, his legs spread in what was usually a very sturdy stance. One arm hung loosely. The other was clasped to his side.

Outside, the faint sound of sirens grew steadily louder. Inside, Harry and Valentina watched as Ahmed took his hand from the growing blood stain on his robe. He stared at it, his thick bushy brows knit in an expression of puzzlement. Then, as majestic and symmetric as a felled sequoia, Ahmed toppled over onto the floor.

Chapter Four

SERGEANT COLE RUSKIN hid his amusement. The floor nurse fidgeted. She looked as if she'd sat on a hornet's nest. She was too stiff, didn't want to bend. The hospital regulations stated that only two visitors were allowed in private rooms at a time. That small number had multiplied in the case of room 432 and the nurse's blood pressure rose.

Old biddy, he thought. She didn't like the idea that Konig had overridden her authority. But what could she do when the police were involved? Just throw a lieutenant out? Maybe so, Ruskin mused, but not Konig. She had made her official complaint and been given the cold shoulder by the doctor in charge. Fuming, the nurse hadn't been back since.

No loss. Ruskin liked pretty women and the nurse hadn't been one of those.

He glanced over to where his superior, Lieutenant Les Konig, leaned back against the wall. The bed with the downed giant separated the two policemen from the other anxious visitors. The wounded man hadn't stirred since his release from the recovery room. They'd removed the bullet and stitched the giant back together. Ruskin watched the quiet, even rise and fall of the broad chest. The man's skin looked darker against the pristine white of the bandages that criss-crossed his torso. Ruskin had every confidence that, should the plethora of visitors irritate the large man, even with his newly treated wound, the giant could toss his guests from the room as easily as an athlete would toss a 16 pound hammer in an Olympic event. Probably more easily.

Ruskin turned his attention back to the lieutenant. Konig was staring thoughtfully at the bronzed face of the big man in the bed. Ahmed Gabbai looked much better than he had lying on the floor at the Crosby house. When Konig and Ruskin had first arrived, it had looked as if they'd be dealing with two corpses. The giant had lain so still, his breathing shallow. When the paramedics arrived he'd come around hissing unpleasant-sounding foreign words at them. Ruskin hadn't any trouble understanding the gist of his complaints, though. He'd felt that way himself when he'd dodged from a bullet the wrong way.

The giant wasn't as easy on the eyes as other occupants of the room. There were three of them. A real mismatched group, Ruskin thought.

The elderly woman in the elegant purple outfit had been checked over by the medics. She had revived quickly from her swoon, refusing a whiff of the pungent smelling salts. While they took pictures and removed the corpse from her living room, Loretta Crosby stayed seated at her kitchen table, a bottle of cleaning disinfectant nearby to combat any lasting dizziness, and a glass of brandy in her hand to restore her. It had worked wonders. Ruskin watched her flit about the room with all the energy of a pigeon sampling spilled popcorn at the zoo. He wondered idly how the serious nature of the events earlier that day had touched the elderly woman. There was a nasty blood stain in the center of her soft, slate-colored living room carpet. Would she hide it with a throw rug? No, he decided. Loretta Crosby would take the opportunity to redecorate.

Right now her concern was for the man in the bed and her quiet granddaughter. Valentina Crosby was very reserved. In her designer jeans and Redskins T-shirt, she reminded Ruskin of his neighbor's kid. Valentina had gorgeous green eyes. Too somber for his taste. Unlike her grandmother, Valentina sat still, her knees together, her feet angled toward the chair legs in a child-like manner. She watched the giant in the bed with fear. For himself or because she was afraid of him? Ruskin hadn't decided. Every once in a while she would turn the ring on her third finger, left hand, fiddling with it. The diamond was a hefty-sized rock. Which man had given it to her? The giant in the bed? He doubted it. But the man who stood staring out the window didn't seem a viable candidate either.

The man with two names. Perhaps it came from dealing with too many crooks who used aliases, but Ruskin was confused about his own reaction to the man. Good-looking, but a bit too theatrical with that stylized, pointed beard. The fellow had produced an identification card covered with graceful stylized Arabian script and a Nevada driver's license. His passport listed him as Harry Smith, and the visiting Yemeni group claimed he was Hadi ibn Dawud al-Bakil, son of a prominent Middle Eastern archaeologist. He'd been uneasy trying to explain the tangled web of a life that made the use of a dual designation logical. Konig had accepted the explanation. Like Ruskin, he had dealt with too many devious characters not to recognize Smith's nervousness as mostly embarrassment.

Unlike the women, Smith didn't appear to be worried about the wounded giant. Perhaps his attitude had something to do with the short guttural phrases the Arab had muttered before being taken into the operating room. Smith had answered in the foreign tongue. Ruskin was sure that he'd recognized the name of God, Allah, frequently in the exchange. Twice since that time Smith had turned to face the east and bowed his head as if in prayer. The hospital records showed that Ahmed Gabbai was of the Muslim faith. Ruskin doubted that Smith was a devotee of the Koran, despite the semi-reverence he'd observed in the vague direction of Mecca. When the police had arrived at the Crosby house, three goblets with brandy residue were sitting on the kitchen table, evidence that not just Mrs. Crosby had been fortified with spirits. Ruskin had recently been stuck in the dentist's office with an old copy of National Geographic magazine. The only thing he remembered from the article he'd read on Arabia was that the followers of Mohammad were death on booze.

Smith's brow was furrowed as he stared, unseeing, at the hospital parking lot. His shoulders were hunched as he stood, hands shoved halfway into his jean pockets.

"Let's go over it once more," Lieutenant Konig requested. Ruskin noted that the girl glanced up, her eyes blank. The lean man at the window turned his head, his expression just shy of malevolent.

"Must we?" Loretta Crosby fluttered to her granddaughter's side.

"Wouldn't it be much more to the point to decide what is to be done? I think we need protection. One of them escaped and may try again. Especially after last night's attempt."

Konig's stance against the wall was nonchalant, almost as if he were unaware of the increased tension in the room. He reached for the pack of cigarettes in the inner pocket of his suit jacket automatically before remembering where he was. "Please," he said. He turned to his sergeant. "What have we got, Ruskin?"

Ruskin took a step forward so that he was no longer a pace behind his chief. He'd known the silence wouldn't last forever. Konig tended to ponder the facts for long stretches of time before deciding he needed to hear them afresh. Ruskin spent a lot of time just waiting for his superior to come out of his trance. Konig usually managed to clear up each problem, even if he took his time doing so.

Ruskin opened his notebook and read. "Unknown man, possibly Arabian nationality ..."

"Yemen," Smith said. "He's from Yemen. I couldn't pinpoint whether his accent was from San'a' or down near Aden, though."

"Yemen, then." Ruskin made a note in his book.

Konig folded his arms across his chest. "If you don't mind, could you tell us again where Yemen is, Mr. Smith? And how you came to be there?"

Smith cast a look of exasperation at the Crosby women. The younger one gave him a tremulous smile of encouragement. Maybe he was wrong, Ruskin mused. Maybe Smith had given her the diamond.

"Yemen is south of Saudi Arabia," Smith explained. "To avoid problems, my father felt it would be expedient for me to use the name he'd given me during my stay there this past year. I am a geologist but I was working with an archaeological team. The contract expired yesterday, which is why I was attached to the visiting exhibit."

"Have you ever seen the dead man before? Or his associate?"

"Not to my knowledge."

Konig nodded and switched gears, taking the interrogation in a different path. "So you are Arabian by birth and Hadi al-Bakil is your real name."

Smith grinned in appreciation of the lieutenant's tactics. His teeth were blindingly white, or appeared to be, set against the sun-browned tone of his skin and the dark frame of his black, close-cut beard. "I was born in Chicago, not in a harem. My name was legally changed to Harry Smith when I was a child. My stepfather adopted me."

Ruskin listened once again to the story. Straight out of one of the romance novels his most recent ex-wife read, he thought. Dawud al-Bakil had been a rather dashing student at the University of Chicago studying Egyptology. He'd met blond, bubble waitress Bunny Ludwig, fallen hard, and married her. When his aristocratic father discovered the couple, the young bride was bought off with a large settlement. It was only later that Bunny discovered she was pregnant. She married Nevada rancher Pete Smith when Harry was three months old.

There were spots in the tale that sounded too pat, too trite to be true. Could any woman be as brainless as Smith painted his mother? He did so with a distinct fondness reflected in his voice. For that matter, could any grown man bend so easily to his father's will as to give up a bride? Obviously Dawud al-Bakil had. But just as clear was Dawud's determination to introduce his son to the heritage of his Bedouin ancestors.

It was extremely sound logic, or appeared to be when Smith related it, to hide his American origins while fulfilling the year-long contract in the Middle East. With trouble brewing regularly on the Persian Gulf, using an Arabian identity made a lot of sense. There were already too many American hostages. Given the same chance, Ruskin decided he would have used an alias himself. Smith had the added benefit of having spent summers in the Yemeni highlands learning Arabian customs, and the idioms of the people.

So he had become Hadi, son of David, of the Bakil family. He'd lived in the family home in San'a' with the recently wounded giant as a companion and bodyguard. Now Smith was back in the States and someone wanted to kill him. It was absurd. The man had taken innumerable precautions for his safety in Yemen but had only been in danger once he set foot on his home soil again.

"Tell me about his cousin," Konig urged. "The one who was attacked."

"Badr." Smith nodded. He took his hands from his pockets, pulled up one of the extra chairs the hospital staff had brought into the room at Konig's request, spinning the armless piece of molded plastic around to straddle it. Smith leaned forward, his arms folded along the back of the chair.

"He's an archaeologist, an epigraphist. That means he reads ancient texts. He was attached to the same excavation unit that I worked with. I didn't see much of him since our specialties were in different areas. He worked with larger fragments, anything with writing on it. My stuff was microscopic, trying to trace a pattern in stone fragments in the makeup of pottery."

"What connection, other than the family one, might there be between the attack on him and the two on you?"

The young woman sat forward in her chair. "Do you think the rest of the visiting delegation is in danger?"

Smith snorted in derision. "Think Val," he urged. "You know the kind of stuff on display. A bit of alabaster, marble, mostly carved stone. Pottery. There wasn't anything I would term a *treasure* in the artifacts from the Marib dig."

Loretta Crosby's white locks bobbed as she agreed. "And the man insisted there was a treasure," she said.

"Not a small one either," Smith mused. "They were quite willing to kill over it."

"But, Harry," Valentina persisted, "how were they going to find this treasure if they killed Badr and you, assuming that you are the only ones who supposedly know about it?"

Konig let them talk. Ruskin waited.

"Think," Valentina urged. "There must be something."

Smith glared at her. "You think I haven't been? Hell, Val, I've racked my brain trying to come up with something. Anything."

"It will come to you, dear," Loretta soothed. "I know it will. In the meantime, you're just too worried about Ahmed and your cousin."

Smith sighed deeply. He turned back to the vigilant policemen. "What's more important right now is the safety of these ladies," he said. "Whoever is after me obviously knows of my ... er ... friendship with them."

Valentina's cheeks reddened slightly at his words. Her eyes dropped to her hands. She twisted the diamond ring.

Her grandmother bounced forward. "I agree, dear. But it is Val who's in more danger. They can use her against you."

"Oh, now, Grandma ..." the young woman protested.

Konig cleared his throat to get their attention. "And why would that be, Mrs. Crosby?"

"Because they were once ..."

"Close," Smith interrupted quickly.

Loretta gave him a frustrated look. "Very close," she said.

"It was a long time ago, Lieutenant," Valentina assured Konig. "I don't think that a long-dead ... er ..." She searched for a neutrally descriptive word and fell back on the one Smith had used. "... friendship has any bearing on this. Harry just happened to be visiting."

"I invited Mr. Smith for lunch," Loretta volunteered. She exchanged a quick conspiratorial glance with the dark-haired young man. "To catch up on old times."

"We were going out for Chinese," Smith said. "Ahmed was against it."

Valentina glared at them both. "Those men were probably following Harry, just waiting for an opportunity. They could just as easily have accosted him at the restaurant or some place else. My grandmother and I have nothing to worry about."

"Val! I don't think that you've ..." Loretta began.

Konig cut her off. "You're absolutely right, Mrs. Crosby," he said, surprising his sergeant. "But so are you, Ms. Crosby. I do agree that the incident at your home was a result of the men following the rented car. If the reason Mr. Smith was shot at last night, then followed today, is linked to the attack on his cousin in Yemen, then there is every reason to believe that whoever is behind these attempts knows your close friendship with Mr. Smith. If they have any reason to believe he would be more inclined to give them the information they seek if you were a hostage, I think you would be in danger."

"But it was over five years ago," Valentina insisted. "There's nothing between us anymore."

Ruskin had been watching Smith and the girl. He didn't believe her rash statement.

"I'm engaged to a wonderful man. Todd McAllister," she said. "He's a junior representative from Minnesota."

Smith's laugh was a bark, quickly cut off. "Minnesota? Hell, Val,

52

you'll freeze your—"

"I'll be perfectly safe with Todd." She frowned at him.

Ruskin knew McAllister. A milquetoast of a man. He wondered
how she had ever gone from an affair with Smith to an engagement
to McAllister. If Valentina cowered with McAllister as her pro-
tector, the fool would be more inclined to do something stupid,
trusting to his political platitudes to take care of any situation. A
determined gunman would blow him away. Just from his short
observation of Smith, Ruskin had decided the man had a cool head
and excellent reflexes. Mrs. Crosby's version of the events at her
home bore out that evaluation.

"Let's not take any chances, shall we, Ms. Crosby?" Lieutenant
Konig said. "I'll assign a patrolman to protect you both, and another
to stay with Mr. Smith."

Smith wasn't having any of it. Ruskin saw the man's dark brows
snap together over his light eyes, like thunder clouds over
Washington's famous reflecting pool. "No, you won't, lieutenant,"
Smith said and got to his feet. "Now that I know Ahmed is okay,
I'm not sitting still. I'd rather be on the road ..."

"Running," Valentina said in derision.

"Damn right, Val. Running as fast as I can. I've got to keep
moving while I try to come up with that missing link. There is
a connection. I just need time for it to surface."

Ruskin watched the man carefully. Smith was wound as tight
as a jammed mainspring on a clock.

"You're not planning on staying in town?" Konig's voice was
deceptively soft. "I would prefer that you did."

Smith gave the lieutenant a cocky grin. "I know you would. But
I'm not. Washington seems a bit too hot at the moment. I'll call
in daily, if you want, to let you know where I am."

Konig considered a moment, his forehead creasing a bit more
deeply than usual, then he agreed. "I'll assign an officer to Mrs. Crosby
and her granddaughter."

There was an air of mutiny in the room. Ruskin could almost
smell it.

Loretta's neatly coiffed white hair shook vehemently. "I don't
think that's a sensible plan," she said. "Then the bad guys will know
we're a weak link."

"The bad guys," Konig mused. His lips twitched. "Then what do you propose, Mrs. Crosby?"

She brightened. "Disappearing," she declared. "That's what Harry's planning to do. We can, too. I have friends I haven't visited in years. And Val ..."

Loretta turned to face her granddaughter, her stance that of a woman girding for battle. "I think Val should go with Harry," she said.

"What!" Valentina and Smith responded in unison.

"It's a bad idea, Loretta," Smith growled.

"How could you, Grandma! If you think that ..."

Konig held his hand up, requesting silence. When they complied, he glanced back at his silent sergeant. Ruskin's pen was poised above his pad, but his lips curved in a grin of amusement. "What do you think Sergeant?" Konig asked.

It wasn't often that the lieutenant asked for an opinion; usually it was when he was sure that his officer would back him up. Ruskin had no problem complying. "If Ms. Crosby can be taken as a hostage and used against Mr. Smith, wouldn't it be better for his peace of mind if she was with him?" he said. Ruskin glanced over at the model slim form of Valentina Crosby. She could do a hell of a lot better than that old stick-in-the-mud McAllister. If she hadn't looked so concerned over Smith's safety, he'd volunteer to protect her himself. Despite Valentina's insistence that Harry Smith was just a man from her past, that she was happily engaged to McAllister, she hadn't convinced Ruskin that she was immune to the tender glances Smith gave her. The lady protested too much.

He'd just have to let another pretty woman slip through his fingers, Ruskin thought. "It would sure ease my mind to have her along if I were in his place," he said, cinching the matter.

Konig nodded in agreement. "It isn't normal procedure," the lieutenant said carefully. "But in this case I think Ms. Crosby should be with you, Smith."

Loretta looked smug as she glanced from one fuming young face to the other.

"I recommend that you don't return to the house," Konig said. "We could send a patrol car for some of your things."

Loretta waved her hand airily. "When on the lam, doesn't one just buy new clothing as it is needed?"

"I wouldn't know," the lieutenant said.

"Plastic, Mr. Konig. As long as the credit line holds out, I can stay hidden," Loretta assured him.

Smith ran a hand along his jaw. He was staring at Valentina thoughtfully. "I suppose we're stuck, Val," he said. "I'll have the car rental place pick up the Olds I left at your house. We can park your car at the airport, and rent another."

"Leave Grandma's Mercedes at the airport?" Valentina cried. "Are you nuts? Do you know what could ..."

Loretta gathered up her purse. "Then you can drop me there," she declared, cheerfully cutting off her granddaughter. "I'll call a few friends and catch the next plane out. Will that suit you, Lieutenant?"

"Perfectly."

Both Smith and Konig glanced down at the still unconscious giant on the bed between them. Ahmed Gabai's breathing was regular, if a bit shallow. He'd been fortunate that the bullet had not torn a vital organ. Even luckier that the assassin hadn't used an automatic weapon. The single shot had felled the big man, but it hadn't done much damage.

"I will assign a man here," Konig said quietly.

Smith met his eyes. "Thank you. I appreciate it."

"Anything else we can do for you?" Konig asked.

Smith's eyes were the clearest blue Ruskin had encountered in a long time. The concern faded from them, replaced with a self-deprecating humor. "Well," Smith drawled, his hand once more rubbing his bristled jaw. "A razor might help. This beard makes me stand out like a Democrat in a Republican caucus."

Sikina, daughter of Zafir al-Rahman, wife of Badr al-Hashid, followed the crowd from the plane, through customs and away from the gates at Kennedy International.

It was exhilarating to be in New York again. She breathed deeply, savoring the stale scents of the terminal. The long dark robes of Islam had been left behind in Yemen. She had worn western clothing beneath her draperies. The concealing black had been discarded in the tiny restroom aboard the plane once they had left

55

the Arabian Peninsula behind. She had no further use for them. She had no intention of ever returning to Yemen.

The money she'd discovered in Badr's belt hadn't been sufficient to finance the trip. It had taken another measure of guile to convince the manager at his bank to give her a large draft. Fortunately, Badr was still unconscious when the man had tried to check with him, to verify the story she had told of being sent to visit her sister for safety while he recovered.

Recovered. Her husband would recover just to spite her. Sikina was still furious that Faraday had not killed Badr. He had made excuses instead, insisting that he had not had the opportunity, that other doctors and hospital staff members had been too near, that the circumstances could not ensure that he would not be suspected.

Eliot Faraday possessed a weakness that she had not suspected before.

Sikina tucked her slim purse beneath her arm and let the crowds sweep her through the terminal. The click of her heels on the tiled flooring echoed the word in her heart. *Free.* At last she was as free as she had been as a girl. No veils, no robes, just the whisper of silk as she strode along.

A number of men looked after her petite form, at the way the light summer dress clung to her voluptuous curves. They lifted their noses slightly, as if to catch the exotic essence of her perfume. Sikina smiled complacently. This was what she had longed for, what she had craved.

It had been unfair of her father to allow her older sister, Fatima, to marry an American, then forbid the same right to her. Zafir, a representative of his country to the United Nations, had made a mistake in bringing his family to New York. The influences that touched his two daughters were contrary to all that he believed under Islam. He had not been prepared for the unwomanly spirit his daughter, Fatima, had shown in her determination to marry Gary Cosgrove. Rather than have his daughter disgrace her family, he had consented to Fatima's marrying her stock-broker.

The same mistake would not be made twice, he had vowed, much to Sikina's chagrin. Although just fifteen, she had already made the acquaintance of pre-med student Eliot Faraday. His fiery-red hair and pale skin had entranced her. Farady's obvious admiration of her had appealed strongly to her budding woman's vanity. When her father had suddenly arrived and withdrawn her from the school, sending her back to relatives in San'a', her memories of Faraday had been all that sustained her lonely hours.

It had been difficult to adjust to the cloistered life in her uncle's household. Within a few months he had arranged for her marriage to her distant cousin, Badr al-Hashid. She had fond memories of her bridegroom-to-be. They had played together as children, along with another cousin, Hadi al-Bakil. She and Fatima had followed the two boys around, hoping to share in their adventures during those summers in Sirwah. Badr had been officious, already interested in sharing his father's work in archaeology. Hadi had been as mysterious and fascinating as a *jinn* with a magic carpet. His ready laugh and American accent had sung out over the hills with a freshness that drew censure from the adults, especially with his impatience at the frequency of Muslim prayer times.

In a way, Faraday had reminded her briefly of Hadi. He too was restless. But outside of that, there was very little similarity between the two men. Faraday's accent was clipped, Hadi's was lazy, almost sensual. Faraday snapped, Hadi purred.

Shut away in her home, surrounded by chattering women, her only contact with men now with her uncle, Sikina had dreamed and wondered. Hadi was also her cousin. What would life have been like if her uncle had chosen him as her mate?

It would never have happened. Hadi's visits to his father had stopped when he reached manhood. He had never embraced Islam. Despite his blood, Hadi was a foreigner, an American. What good had it done to dream when she knew her fate was sealed? Sikina, like a devoted Islamic woman, had bowed to the rule of her male relatives, submitted to the magpie enthusiasm of the women who painted her palms with henna and decked her in bride jewels. Badr would be no worse than any other man chosen for her. She would endure.

The years had crept by. Sikina had alternately cursed and praised Allah for making her barren. Children would only have bound her more tightly to a life she despised. Her husband was gone frequently, his involvement in various archaeological digs taking him from his office at the museum as well as away from her arms.

She had not minded. She had her house, her friends, her memories.

Then she had run into Eliot Faraday in the marketplace.

He had not recognized her. How could he with the enveloping black robes and veil disguising her? It had been nearly ten years since she had met him. She had been a girl then. Now she was a woman.

Sikina had looked for him again, carefully covering her interest from the other women around her. Surreptitiously, she had discovered where he lived, where he worked, had written to him, had arranged to meet him. And they had become lovers.

It hadn't mattered to Sikina that her life would be forfeit if they were discovered. She thrived on the danger. She longed for the freedom of Western life. Letters from her sister, Fatima Cosgrove in New York City, only made her hunger the more.

The plot had begun to form the night she overheard Badr talking with a nervous man in the garden. He sent her to bed, his voice sharp, irritated—whether with her or the sudden appearance of the filthy stranger, she didn't know. Her curiosity got the better of her as she lay waiting for Badr to join her, and she stole back to wait in the shadows. It was then that she heard the magic word: treasure.

A hoard of the ancients, the stranger insisted. The spoils of an empire older than time.

Her husband, Badr, held something in his hands. His touch was reverent, his voice hoarse with emotion. She had never seen him exhibit such enthusiasm over an object, even over an artifact. For surely that was what the unknown item was. Sikina wished she dared steal closer. The light of a single lamp seemed to glint on it.

Gold, she thought. Her dark eyes gleamed as brightly as the unknown piece of history in Badr's grasp. Gold.

Badr laughed, his voice low and throaty. "If what you say is true, evil one," he said to the man in the ragged robes, "then the riches that await us are those of a queen's cache. A royal tomb."

The beggar-thief grinned, his lips stretched to reveal ghat-stained teeth. "Then you will pay, *efendi?* You are pleased?"

"More than pleased," Badr said and wrapped the mysterious artifact within the rag of cloth the thief had used to disguise it.

The ragged man looked sly a moment then let his face return to its obeisant cast. "And it will be safe here, *efendi?*"

"It will be safe," Badr agreed. "But not here, evil one. The curse of the Unifier will guard it well in my stead."

Sikina quietly made her way back to her chamber. She sat among the bedding hugging her knees in excitement. *The Unifier.* She had not heard that name since her childhood. Her mind went back to the last time she had enjoyed a summer of unfettered childhood, the final time she and Fatima had played with Badr and Hadi at the summer house in Sirwah.

The boys were cocky, proud of the fact that they were male, and thus superior under Allah. They were older than the two little girls and had enjoyed boasting of a secret, something they had discovered. The Treasure of the Unifier, they had called it, and been very smug about it. But Sikina had spied on them as they drew the map, had watched from her hiding place as they poured over it before they divided it for safekeeping.

Her husband still carried that fragment with him. Or he had until Faraday removed it from his money belt.

She doubted that the childish treasure with the grand title had amounted to much more than the odd bits and pieces that boys collected. But the fact that Badr had removed his share of the map from his wallet to safety within the concealed money belt foretold its new worth. If Hadi still carried his half, and she obtained that scrap of yellowed paper, the wealth of an ancient monarch would be hers. The key was in Hadi's map, for it was on the missing section that she believed the location of the treasure trove was marked. If the "Unifier" guarded Badr's new find, that meant that he had hidden it in Sirwah, in the secret hiding place he had once shared with Hadi al-Bakil.

Sikina smiled to herself, gaining a few more startled but complimentary looks from the men she passed. Soon, she told herself as she stepped up to the counter of the commuter airline. Soon, the treasure would be all hers.

The uniformed man at the computer terminal looked bemused when he met her shining dark eyes. "Can I help you?" His voice pleaded that he be allowed the pleasure.

Sikina's expression was as complacent as that of a pampered Persian cat. "Perhaps you can," she purred. "When will the next flight leave for Washington, D.C.?"

Chapter Five

VALENTINA BLINKED IN the first glare of the sun. It had dispelled the lovely dream too soon. She frowned, her eyes still closed, and willed the fantasy to return. Elusive, the pleasant dream refused to cooperate. In it an unkempt, dark haired man had cherished her, and she had been in love with him. Illogically so, she thought. After all, Todd McAllister had carefully groomed blond hair.

She moaned in disgust as the sun intruded on her once more. She moved to turn over in bed, to pull the blankets over her head. But there was no comfortable bed, no soft, warm blankets.

Then she remembered. Reluctantly Valentina opened her eyes to stare at the dashboard of the rented Geo Prizm.

Out of the dream and into the nightmare. Next to her in the slightly reclined driver's seat, Harry Smith slept on, a baseball cap over his face.

They were parked at a rest area off the Interstate. Where, Valentina wondered? Wheeling, West Virginia, had been the last town she remembered. It had been long past midnight when they'd crossed the river there. That meant this was Ohio.

There were a number of tall old trees at the stop. Birds, fresh from their early breakfasts of worms, shrilled happily. Discussing the latest peccadillos of their neighbors, Valentina supposed. That's what it had always sounded like to her. A good reason to avoid early morning risings.

This one couldn't be avoided, though. She had caught just enough sleep to now find that the once comfortable bucketseat had grown sharp corners and inflexible springs.

Valentina got out of the car and closed the door softly so as not to disturb Harry. She stretched and shivered slightly in the dew-damp air.

She wondered where her grandmother had finally landed. Had she gone to New York City as Valentina had urged? Or had she chosen San Francisco as Harry suggested? Knowing her grandmother, the destination would be neither.

The Mercedes had been reluctantly left at Washington's National Airport. Harry, with Loretta backing him up, had insisted they needed a car that wouldn't be recognized, though the bright red Geo Prizm he'd rented didn't seem such a neutral choice. At her grandmother's urging they hadn't waited to see her off, thus enabling Loretta to keep her destination secret, a move that made Valentina very suspicious of her grandmother's plans. Harry immediately headed north, working his way toward Interstate 270.

Dinner had been a quick turkey sandwich at a convenience store, eaten en route. Twilight was already in its final stages when the Prizm took the loop onto Interstate 70 heading west.

If Harry had a destination in mind, it certainly wasn't the one Valentina had overheard him mention to the attendant at the car rental desk. "Charlotte," he'd drawled, his voice purposefully dropping into a seductive sounding baritone. God, she hated it when he did that. Once it had made her jealous as hell. Now, thank goodness, she was immune to that caressing voice, Valentina assured herself. She was along for this ride only because the police had insisted. But the tone of his voice brought a speculative gleam into the eyes of the girl behind the counter. Valentina could almost see her shiver with pleasure.

Charlotte, North Carolina, was a *long* way from wherever they were now. So where were they going? Other than west, that is. The only place she could think of in that direction was Nevada—home. Harry really wouldn't be that obvious though. Or would he?

Valentina wondered as she strolled toward the unattractive block building that housed the relief station.

She took her time, splashing her face, hoping the sharp sting of the cold water would put some color in her face. Once she hadn't used cosmetics. Now she felt naked without them. She nearly broke her comb trying to get her hair in some order. It had looked better longer, and been easier to take care of, too. Then she had twisted it back into a pony tail when she was in a hurry, which had been most of the time. Her new shorter cut took a blow dryer, mousse, and spritz to look decent. She scrubbed at her teeth with a water-dampened finger, then stared at her hands. Three carefully cultivated nails were gone. The weeks of self control had been for nothing. Since Harry Smith had shown up in her life again, she'd gone back to gnawing on her nails. Todd would be angry. As if he'd been the one who'd worked so hard. Sometimes she could just ...

Valentina shook herself. She loved Todd. She was going to marry him. If she had to be ticked off with anyone, it should be that damn Harry Smith.

He was awake and leaning against the side of the car when she returned. His eyes were a bit shadowed with sleeplessness but she'd seen him look that way before when he'd had a paper due, or during finals week when he was swamped, grading freshman exams for the geology lab classes. Back then she'd found that heavy lidded look extremely sexy.

She did now, too.

The baseball cap was pushed to the back of his head allowing his wavy brown-black hair to spill forward over his brow. Although he'd shaved off the *Arabian Nights* beard, he'd kept the mustache. It drooped around his mouth, making Valentina think of a Mexican bandit rather than of Scheherazade's Sinbad. With his hair falling in those disgustingly beautiful blue eyes, Harry didn't look any different than he had five years ago. He grinned, his teeth an impossible white that nearly glinted in the early morning sun.

Lord, he looked good.

"Morning, gorgeous," Harry greeted. Just as he had every day all those years ago.

It was impossible not to remember how they'd spent their first waking moments back then. Once the clock radio turned on, often blasting them with one of the current top ten selections from Billboard, Harry had always gathered her close. She could almost feel the scratch of his mustache against the nape of her neck, almost feel the soft tickle of his breath before ...

Valentina forced her mind away from memories. Just to be safe, she kept the Prizm between them.

"I don't feel gorgeous," Valentina growled. "In fact, I would kill for a toothbrush and a bottle of mouthwash." She glared at him. "And a shower."

Harry reached in the open window and retrieved his sunglasses from the dashboard. "Patience, honey. We had to put a few miles under our belts last night."

"I'd prefer breakfast under mine," Valentina said and glared at him again, determined to show him she hadn't forgiven the past, even if she was forced to endure his company now. Her own image scowled back at her in duplicate from the mirrored lenses of his glasses. Damn! It made her feel as if she were in a Doublemint commercial. "Where are we, anyway?" she demanded.

Harry looked around at the tall trees, at the green carpet of grass. "Ohio?"

"Where in Ohio?"

"Somewhere in the middle, I think."

Valentina sighed.

"Val," he drawled, drawing her name out in the same caressing tone he'd used on the girl at the car rental booth. "We're outside of Columbus. Actually past it."

"And where are we going?"

"To breakfast?"

It wasn't the answer she wanted, but after the rather unsatisfactory sandwich the night before, it was an acceptable answer. Valentina pulled open the car door and dropped back into her seat. "How far?"

Harry tossed the baseball cap into the back seat and slid beneath the wheel once more. "A little way yet. I want to reach Vandalia."

"There's a five-star breakfast parlor there?" Valentina pulled her seatbelt into place and snapped it.

The Prizm's motor turned over and purred quietly. "More importantly, there's an airport there," Harry said.

"So we're going to fly now?"

"Nope." He grinned over at her and backed out of the parking spot. His arm draped along the back of her seat as he turned to look through the rear window. "We're going to rent another car."

At least breakfast had come first. Valentina sat across from Harry in the booth at Frisch's Restaurant, marvelling at the amount of food on his plate. He had ordered two eggs (sunny side up) a stack of three large pancakes, plus sausage and bacon, orange juice, and coffee. She watched him pour a generous dose of maple syrup over the hotcakes, and felt a tinge of envy. As hungry as she was, Valentina had kept Todd's admonitions in mind and ordered fruit and wheat toast. Her glass of tomato juice didn't have quite the kick a whiff of Harry's coffee had, but it was better for her. At least Todd insisted it was.

Harry looked up from cutting off the end of a sausage and intercepted the lustful look as Valentina stared at his plate. "You want a bite?" he offered.

"No, no. I'm fine," she insisted. But the look she gave her bowl of grapefruit pieces was malevolent.

His lips twitched in amusement then he popped the sausage in his mouth, savoring the longed-for flavor of pork.

"Have you thought about that treasure any more?" Valentina stabbed a grapefruit section.

"Yeah." Harry sopped up extra syrup on a fork full of pancake. "No luck. Yet. It'll come to me."

"I hope so." She bit into the fruit and wrinkled her nose at the tart taste. "Tell me about your cousin. The one that was attacked in San'a.'"

"Badr." Harry smiled down at his plate. "Strange guy in some ways. Totally devoted to archaeology. You'd understand that, Val." A piece of bacon disappeared before he continued. "But the pressure to match up to his father's work has turned him into a fanatic."

Valentina forced another piece of fruit past her lips. "In what way?"

"Well, Yussuf, his father, is a top authority on pre-Islamic cultures in Arabia. The caravan routes, in particular. They were well established already when the empires of Egypt were just rising. Some of Yussuf's most admired findings deal with dates back farther than three thousand years before the present."

"The tenth century B.C.?"

"You're behind the times, Val. The preferred dating method now is non-sectarian. Especially in a Muslim world. We use *before present*. But you're right about the century. Yussuf's work at the

Temple of 'Awwam in Sirwah kept all of us near the site when I was a kid and visited in the summers. Badr wasn't happy about being in his father's shadow then and it still irks him."

Valentina gave up on her grapefruit and nibbled a slice of dry toast. She stared at Harry's eggs with longing.

"I'm not sure when it started," Harry said and paused to finish off his pancakes. "There was a long stretch there when I didn't visit Dad. He'd gotten a position at the Cairo Museum. Dad's great love is Egypt even if he did work in Yemen for years. Anyway, it wasn't as convenient for him or for me to visit. He never married after the fiasco with my mother, and didn't have relatives in Cairo to help take care of me. Besides, I was a teenager by then and more interested in having my own car than in being stuck in a Middle Eastern city with nothing to do."

He looked around for the waitress and waved her down before returning to his story. "A side of hash browns," he requested, then looked at Valentina's half-empty bowl of fruit. "Need anything else, Val?"

She felt very saintly refusing the offer. But her eyes strayed to Harry's plate often as one entree after another disappeared.

"Where was I? Oh, yeah. Badr." Harry took a sip of coffee, gathering his thoughts. "Badr aced things in school. He could read Sumerian backwards when he was thirteen so I wasn't surprised when he decided to specialize in written languages. Translating the adventures of Gilgamesh didn't satisfy Badr though. He started scouring the archives, looking for any mention of the Queen of Saba. Bilqis. She's supposed to have lived three millenia ago in the Marib area. There are legends but no proof. Badr is determined to find that proof."

Valentina leaned back in her seat. "You think he might have found something? That this proof is the treasure?"

"Could be. Yet I doubt it." The hash browns arrived. The waitress lingered, filling Harry's coffee cup.

When they were alone again, Valentina had a few more questions ready. "Why do you doubt it? Wouldn't an artifact that old be worth something? Even if it's just a clay tax tablet or something, it's still valuable."

"To an academic. To a collector, maybe. But worth killing for? It has to be more, Val."

She pondered a moment. "Wouldn't other archaeologists be involved though? There are always professionals as well as volunteers and diggers on a site. If Badr found something, something that wasn't in an archive somewhere, he wouldn't be the only one in danger."

Harry washed down a mouthful of potatoes with a quick gulp of coffee. "Only one trouble with that. Badr isn't always on the up and up with his discoveries. He hasn't been caught buying from thieves, but I know he's dealt with them before. If a man brought him something, sold him some information—well—there would be no official team involved."

"Then in that case, Harry," Valentina pursued, "why did someone try to kill you?"

He frowned, his dark brows looking almost as fierce as Ahmed's. "I don't know."

They both stared at the table in thought. Valentina trying not to give in to the temptation to eat Harry's last piece of bacon; Harry wondering if he'd ever make the connection between the attack on Badr and the two attempts on his own life.

"How come you never told me about your real father when we were together?" Valentina asked softly. Her eyes stayed lowered, as if she were concentrating on the patterns the condensation on her water glass created on the table surface.

Harry leaned back and spread his hands in a gesture of helplessness. "Ah, well, it didn't actually come up."

"It should have," she said. "You had the perfect opening. I was an archaeology major."

"Cliff-dwelling Indians and camel-driving Bedouins aren't exactly the same kind of study, Val. Besides, I didn't want you to love me because I had archaeological blood in my veins. I wanted you to love me for myself."

She moved the glass, adding to the pattern of damp circles. "I did. Then."

Harry stared at her hands, at the sparkling diamond ring on her finger. "Val ..."

But Valentina didn't want to talk about the past, their shared past. "Tell me what it was like in Yemen when you were a kid."

"It was ..." He grinned ruefully to himself. "... different," he said. "I guess I was five the first time I went. Dad met me at the airport and took me back to my cousin's house. My memories of that place are pretty vague. Children spend most of their time with the women. In my case, I also had a tutor to teach me the language. Fortunately, young kids catch on fast. It wasn't long before I was Badr's constant companion. We were pretty much of an age. Since both our fathers were archaeologists, we had something in common."

Harry's voice took on a dream-like quality as he thought back to those days in a distant land. "What I really remember though, is the stories the women told at night," he said. "Tales of evil *jinns*, clever thieves, and beautiful maidens. They loved to tell me a story called *The Foreign Bride*. Probably because my mother wasn't one of them."

"What happens in it?"

Harry laughed and reached for the check. "She marries a prince, has a son, loses him to adventure, then is happily reunited with him when he wins the girl of his dreams. Come on. We'd better get back on the road."

The two women paused, as if posing in the doorway. The uniformed policewoman glanced toward Konig's empty office, then down a row of desks to where Ruskin sat pounding on a keyboard, filling out a report. The petite woman at her side waited patiently, her exotic features adding to the air of mystery that seemed to surround her still form.

A ripple went through the room as one man after another looked up and was temporarily bemused by the captivating face and generous curves of the visitor. Ruskin felt the change in the atmosphere, heard the slowing of office chatter. When he looked up, he felt as he had when he'd been a kid and hit his first home run —stunned, disoriented and quaking inside. He'd always been partial to pretty women. But he'd never experienced such a gut-wrenching pull toward any female before. Not even with his two ex-wives. He watched in fascination as the women headed for his desk.

Officer Patsy Christopher had never sought any man's notice. She was as broad across the shoulders as any of her male counterparts, and, since being transferred to a desk, twice as wide across the beam. She walked like a man, striding forward without the faintest twitch of her generous hips. Even her voice was gruff when she spoke, which was usually in a short bark, like a drill sergeant.

"Ruskin," she snapped. "Maybe you can help Mrs. Hashid here." Then she turned and quick-marched away, leaving the vision standing at his desk.

No other woman could have contrasted so sharply as this beauty did with Officer Christopher. Beneath the uncomplimentary glare of fluorescent lights, her upswept dark hair gave off a luminous blue glow. Her face was delicate, with elegant cheekbones, deep set eyes, and a full sensual mouth. Her skin was dusky, like that of a society doll who had recently begun to sun herself at a poolside, the tone warm, yet far from dark.

Ruskin tried to keep his attention on the visitor's face, on the alluring curve of her lips. When she moved, her silver gray dress whispered and appeared to ripple over her breast. The deep cut neckline drew his eyes, but he forced them back to her face. The woman had noticed though. Her lips curved knowingly.

"I'm Sergeant Cole Ruskin," he said and held out his hand, gesturing toward the chair to the right of his desk. "What can I do for you, Mrs. Hashid?"

She studied him a moment, then sat down, crossing her legs. The silk skirt sighed and slithered, exposing a good deal of shapely thigh.

Sloe eyes, that's what hers were, Ruskin decided. Dark as sin and sheltered by the longest, thickest lashes he'd ever seen.

"I was hoping for word of my cousin," she said.

Her voice was as smooth and husky as a telephone solicitor. And a lot more promising.

"He was with the visiting Yemeni archaeological exhibit," she continued. "I am seeking his protection. You see, my husband was attacked by an assassin a few days ago and seriously harmed. He feared for my safety and sent me to join Hadi until he recovers."

Ruskin nodded. "Understandable," he said.

"Unfortunately, when I arrived the commission told me that Hadi disappeared late yesterday afternoon." She leaned forward, her eyes entreating. "Can you help me find him?"

Ruskin cleared his throat, annoyed at himself for being so fascinated with her. He drew back, away from her, as if putting space between them would exorcise his attraction to her. "Yesterday?

I'm afraid I can't help you, ma'am. Now if it had been 72 hours, we could file a missing person report. There just hasn't been enough of a time lapse yet. I wish I could ..."

She didn't appear disturbed with his answer. In fact, she smiled softly at him. "You misunderstand me, Sergeant. If Hadi has disappeared, he is in hiding. Perhaps there has already been an attempt on his life as well." Her lashes dipped. "I am not familiar with the ways of men, but I believe that when there is a treasure to be won, an evil man will overcome all difficulties that are placed in his way."

Treasure. He made the connection now. The man with two names. Smith.

"What would your husband's full name be, Mrs. Hashid?"

"My husband? I do not ... Ah, of course. You wish to verify my identity. He is Dr. Badr ibn Yussuf al-Hashid of the San'a' Museum in Yemen. Perhaps you have heard of him?"

Oh, he'd heard of him alright, Ruskin mused. Not in the context she implied, however. "And your cousin's?"

"Hadi ibn Dawud al-Bakil," she said. Her voice was more like the coo of a dove than that of a flesh and blood woman. "Though I believe he is known here as Harry Smith."

Ruskin leaned back in his chair. "I'm afraid there has been trouble, Mrs. Hashid," he said. "Your cousin has been attacked. Twice."

Her back straightened in shock. "Oh, no! Is Hadi ...?" she let the question hang unfinished between them.

"He's fine." Ruskin tried not to look at the way her dress pulled tightly as her breast rose and fell in agitation. "He's in hiding, as a precautionary measure."

She rustled in her seat. "Then I must join him. Immediately!" she insisted. "It is my husband's wish."

Ruskin sighed deeply. "I realize that, but it's impossible."

"I am ..." she paused. Her eyes glistened with tears. "You see, I am in danger also," she whispered huskily. "Please take me to where my cousin is."

Ruskin felt helpless. He had handled weeping women before, those who'd just lost a loved one, those who'd just been attacked, those who'd just been busted for a crime. He'd thought his skin was tough enough to weather these emotional storms. There was something about this gorgeous creature that made him forget he was a professional.

"I can't," he said. "Not because I don't think it is a good idea for you to join him. It's just that ... well, we don't know where he is."

Sikina held her temper in control. She stared at the police sergeant as if stupefied. He had reacted just as she wished, nearly slobbering in his eagerness to please her. Everything had gone as she wished. If the trio of fools in her employ had followed her instructions, the missing section of the map would be hers now. But they were men and had not seen fit to take directions from a woman. They had probably thought to find the treasure themselves, pushing her aside as insignificant. Instead they had failed twice and one of them was dead.

"I do not understand," she said slowly. "You have lost Hadi?"

"Not exactly. He's on the road. We expect him to call in any time now."

No wonder Sattam and Iz'al had been unsuccessful in locating Hadi. It had not occurred to them that her cousin would leave town.

Resting her brow against her hand, as if the sergeant's news had been too much for her to bear, Sikina watched him from beneath the blind of her lowered lashes. He was not unattractive. His eyes were as docile as those of an aging camel; his build as wiry as a marketplace thief. There were strands of gray in his chestnut hair and deep lines at the corners of his mouth. The soft knit of his dark green sport shirt was creased beneath his shoulder holster. A light-weight, beige jacket was draped over the back of his chair. Wearing it, she supposed he would look like any other Washington resident headed for the golf course.

"I see," she said and raised tragic eyes to meet his concerned ones. Her voice was a wavery whisper. "What am I to do, Mr. Ruskin?"

The sergeant shifted uncomfortably in his chair. Then, as if making a decision, he squared his shoulders. "I'll tell you what I can do, Mrs. Hashid ..."

"Oh, please," she urged, her tone throaty and full of promise. "My name is Sikina."

Chapter Six

ELIOT FARADAY TILTED the lamp shade until the light shone directly on the piece of paper in his hand. It had taken a good hour of sorting through Badr al-Hashid's desk to find the scrap. He hoped his time had been well spent.

In another room Mohammad was methodically destroying Sikina's once pristine home. The brightly woven rugs had been pulled up, tossed aside in the effort to cover her own involvement in the attempt on her husband's life. Richly colored pillows were ripped open to spill their feather stuffing about the floor. The shutters were still tightly closed, and would stay that way until the authorities arrived, or Badr al-Hashid recovered and returned home.

A rumble of sound echoed in the room as Mohammad sent a shelf of books tumbling. Faraday looked up only briefly, then turned his attention back to his find.

It was a copy of a bank draft. The amount was suspiciously large, but that only assured Faraday that he'd found the clue for which he searched. It had been written the week before, for cash. A notation showed the sum was intended as payment to a Nahar Aflaq.

Faraday grinned to himself. Sikina had not thought to search for the key to the treasure here in San'a'. She had locked on to the existence of the map and was single-minded in her pursuit of it. He had arranged for three men to assist her. Men who ultimately took their orders from him rather than Sikina. They had left for the States the same day he had located Hadi al-Bakil. He had been furious at first. The man had been within their grasp right there in the city. But Sikina had purposefully delayed putting the plan in effect until Bakil had left the country. Faraday was suspicious. Did she really think that he would gather up the artifacts when they found the cache and run back to her arms, eager to turn over the ill-gotten fortune to her? For all her sly manipulations, the little tramp was amazingly trusting.

He had other plans, and they didn't involve tying himself to a harem woman. Despite her schooling in America, that was really all that Sikina was now. She might long for what she saw as her sister's freedom in America, but she wasn't mentally equipped to live the life after which she lusted. There would always have to be a man to run things for her. The position didn't suit Faraday. And neither did Sikina. She had merely been a pleasant diversion. He would find the treasure without her.

Faraday folded the paper neatly in half and pocketed it. Then he pulled each drawer of the desk out, flinging it to the far side of the room. A shower of files and documents filled the air before drifting down to blanket the floor. In quick succession other drawers followed until he had destroyed the former neatness of the office.

The doctor was not the man with the fiery-red hair. Badr's fuzzy mind concentrated on the white-jacketed physician as he checked the knife wound, then rebandaged it. Where was he? And how much time had passed since he'd met Nahar in the *suq*? He had been attacked there. By whom? And when had it been?

"You were lucky," the strange doctor mused in a stilted Arabian dialect. His phrasing resembled the written word, rather than the spoken idioms of the people. "Damn lucky. But the wound is healing nicely. If Faraday agrees, I would think you'll be going home in a day or two."

Faraday. So that was the name of the man who had insulted his honor, who had seduced his wife. He had not known the identity of her lover until the doctor had made a telling comment to his assistant, in the mistaken belief that Badr was asleep.

The new doctor picked up the chart at the foot of the bed and studied it. "Hmm. Don't understand why he's kept you sedated though. Curious." The man smiled faintly, then muttered an aside in English, apparently unaware that his patient understood every word. "Unless you've got a pretty wife who visits you. That would be Eliot's style." The doctor hung the chart back on its hook and reverted to Arabic once more. "If you need something to sleep, just ask for it. Otherwise I'm not prescribing any medication."

Badr kept his eyes closed, ignoring the ravings of the man in the next bed.

Badr's ribs were stiff, the pain sharp when he tried to move, but Allah would help him endure. Badr waited until the doctor had moved on to the next ward, then pushed himself upright. His own clothing and the money belt were gone. Dimly he recalled that Sikina had been there. She would have taken his things, the currency in particular. Had she taken the map? There was no reason to suppose she had. Sikina knew nothing of the golden plaque he'd hidden in Sirwah, or of the glory finding the tomb of Queen Bilqis would bring him.

The clothing of the man in the adjacent bed lay temporarily forgotten on the chair nearby. Badr reached for it, pulling on the wide flowing trousers first, then the loose, flowing robe. The items smelled of camel, goat, and sweat. They were filthy, but they fit. The man in the bed protested faintly when Badr took his worn sandals as well.

The call for prayer had long passed when Badr, dressed in the beggar's rags, let himself out a side door into the alley. Shadows were thick and concealing. Slowly, he made his way through the streets, back to his own tall, stone house. When pain forced him to stop and rest, the thought of the revenge he would take on his wife, Sikina, and her lover gave him the strength to move on. The unfamiliar doctor's light-hearted words beat with the force of a drum in his mind. Not only had he discovered the identity of the man with whom Sikina had betrayed him, but it was known by others.

They laughed at him now, Badr thought. His step quickened as he neared the narrow street on which he lived. He pressed the wound in his side, willing the pain to ease. No one would ridicule Badr al-Hashid for long. They would toast him, praise his actions. For when he, Badr al-Hashid was finished exacting punishment, Faraday and his faithless wife, Sikina, would be dead.

Badr stumbled within the entranceway to his house. It was shut tight. Was she entertaining the fiery-haired man in his home, in his bed? Badr flung open the door. It struck the wall with the force of a monsoon. The echo came back to him through the empty rooms. Furnishings lay in broken disorder. Driven by his quest for revenge, Badr visited each floor, each corner. The spilled clumps of feathers rose and fell softly back to the floor as he passed. Room after room he checked, nearly unconscious of the destruction he found everywhere. In Badr's mind there was only one reason for despair. Allah had not guided his steps. Sikina and her lover were not there.

"Gone!" the doctor shouted. "He can't be! Hashid had a knife wound! He was in no shape to be released. He was ... hell!"

Valentina woke up to find the newest rental, a silver-tone Toyota Corolla, parked near the golden double arch of a McDonald's. Harry was nowhere in sight.

She straightened the lime green T-shirt she'd found at the gift shop at the Vandalia airport. It had a delicate bouquet of flowers painted on the front and hung loosely on her slim frame. There hadn't been much in the way of a change of clothes available, just a rack of shirts. She'd gotten Harry one with a cartoon figure of Bart Simpson on it. In his desire to keep constantly on the move, Harry was being just as obnoxious as Bart, so why not broadcast the fact? She'd bought a new comb and a couple packages of Tic Tac breath mints since the shop didn't run to toothbrushes.

She was trying to decide whether to go look for Harry when he came out of the restaurant carrying two bags of food.

"Hi, sleepyhead. Have a nice nap?" He pulled open the driver's door and passed her a sack.

Valentina took it and peered inside. "Yeah. Where are we?"

"Terre Haute, Indiana. Almost at the Illinois border."

She reached into the bag and pulled out two chocolate milk shakes. It wasn't what Todd would want her to eat, of course, but keeping to his strict died had caused her to lose ten pounds over the last three months. Valentina knew her grandmother worried about her health. She'd offered to fix special meals, take Valentina out to expensive restaurants, anything to counter the drop in weight. Todd had frowned and merely pointed out that all Valentina had to do was eat more of the things that were good for her. She could learn to eat more vegetables, develop a taste for fish. Well, she hadn't been able to do either. That kind of diet was fine for people who liked the narrow range of acceptable foods. But she wasn't one of them. Would never be one of them.

Valentina drew in her breath, savoring the smells coming from the other bag. Harry handed her a styrofoam box. "I got you a double cheeseburger," he said. "It was your favorite once. If you want something else, Val, just let me know."

Her mind told her to send him back in for a nice neutral salad. Her mouth watered just at the thought of a hamburger.

Mentally, Valentina consigned Todd McAllister and his yuppie diet to hell. "This is fine."

It was more than fine. It was heaven. She took a bite, her eyes closed in ecstasy. She took a sip of the shake. Pure frozen velvet going down. Half the sandwich was gone before her system rebelled.

Valentina put the burger down quickly and clutched a napkin to her lips. Her face took on a green tinge. "Excuse me," she mumbled and hurried inside the building.

When she came out of the women's restroom, Harry was relieved to see her color was back to normal. Perhaps a little white yet, but she wasn't sick. He put an arm around her shoulders and guided her out of the restaurant to the car. "Honey, I'm sorry," he said. "I didn't know."

She waved his apology away and popped a handful of Tic Tacs in her mouth. "It's not your fault. How were you to know I hadn't had beef or fried food in months? I'm fine now. It's psychosomatic, anyway. You've been away from this kind of food longer and you aren't sick."

"Yeah, but ..."

Valentina gave him a weak smile. "I could do with another milk shake—I think," she said. "Vanilla this time. I've got to work my way back to junk food a little more slowly."

Harry swore at himself silently. Couldn't she see that he was concerned? It didn't matter what she said, if he hadn't been so determined to prove to himself that Valentina hadn't changed in five years, he would have asked her what she wanted. Instead he'd plunged ahead, ordering the things he remembered as her favorites.

Damn fool, that's what he was. Harry mentally kicked himself. Of course she'd changed. He'd changed. He wasn't the ass he'd been then. All she had to do was give him the opening and he was ready to explain the compromising position she'd found him in with ... with ... Hell, he couldn't even remember the girl's name! Some undergraduate who'd come to his office at Fong Hall needing help with her block diagrams of left strike-slip faulting. He'd explained it and gone on to sketch anticlines and synclines and other types of formations caused by earthquakes. He hadn't thought anything about the time. Toward the end of every semester there were always students who panicked about drawing geological maps on their finals. But this girl had timed her entrance well. The rest of the department had gone, some headed for home, others catching a quick dinner before their evening classes. She'd surprised him by suddenly dropping down in his lap and kissing him. And that had been when Valentina walked in.

It had been little comfort to find the girl who'd ruined his relationship with Val hadn't tried to learn a thing about drawing maps. To be safe, he'd handed her exam to another graduate assistant to grade. She'd flunked the course without any assistance from him.

But Valentina had already disappeared. With only three weeks to go in the semester, she'd packed her bags and withdrawn from school, while he was nursing a hangover at Denny's apartment, working up his courage to go home to her. Finishing work for his own degree had kept him from following Valentina. It had been his last semester. He'd taken his comprehensive exams, gotten his degree, and decided that he didn't need a temperamental woman in his life.

He'd been wrong. Nothing had been quite the same without Valentina. So he'd drifted from one short-term geologic position to another. It had only been this last year in Yemen, with plenty of time to think that he'd decided to stop the unproductive circles his life was following. He thought he'd found a special niche at last, a way to combine his fascination with geology and the nagging attraction of archaeology. In the fall he'd be a student once more, this time working on his doctorate in archaeology.

Everything had been planned, plotted, and praised. His father Dawud had made a special trip from Cairo to congratulate him on the decision. His mother and stepfather had processed all the paperwork in the States in his absence. He'd felt he was back on track again.

Now Valentina had walked back into his life, and that track seemed far too narrow a gauge to content him.

How could he hope to win her away from this Todd McAllister, if he continued to do stupid things like making her sick? The answer was simple. He couldn't. McAllister had the upper hand. It was evident in the sparkle of the diamond ring on Valentina's hand. Some how, some way, some time during this mad dash across the country he would find a way to win her back. And if he didn't?

Harry paid for the vanilla shake (large size) and pushed that doubt away. The road to success wasn't paved with "ifs." He may not know the woman Valentina had become, but his knowledge of the girl she'd been was intimate. She couldn't have changed that much.

He was relieved to see Valentina's eyes weren't as clouded as they'd been. She actually smiled at him and savored the milk shake with simple pleasure.

"We've got one more stop before we leave here, honey," he told her, starting the car once more.

"A shopping mall?"

Her sense of humor had returned, Harry was pleased to note.

"I'd gladly kill for a change of clothes," Valentina said. "A new shirt wasn't enough."

He reached over and covered her hand with his. Unfortunately it was the one sporting the diamond. "Not yet. I promise you a shopping spree when we get where we're going. My treat."

"Damn right it's your treat." Valentina hadn't moved her hand. She let it lie beneath his on the seat. "I've got much more expensive tastes than I used to have. It's gonna cost you dearly, Harry."

He grinned, then reluctantly released her hand and pulled back out on the street. "Furs and diamonds?"

"Lord, no. Do you know what those environmentalists do to fur coats? They spray-paint them!"

"Okay," he agreed. "I'll only offer you road-kills. What about diamonds?"

Valentina actually chuckled, her voice low and, he hoped, carefree.

"Diamonds? Just pieces of rock. Remember? You drummed that into my head once."

"Self defense, Val. My budget only ran to glass back then."

"So did my taste, Harry."

She'd almost said his name with that tender inflection he remembered. It cheered Harry considerably. Gave him hope.

As if Valentina realized her slip, she abandoned the light teasing. "What's the stop we have to make?"

"Telephone."

"To call ahead for reservations?"

"To check with Konig in Washington."

"Oh. What are you going to tell him?"

Harry smiled ahead at the traffic. "Just what you know, honey. That we're about to head into Illinois."

She had to be satisfied with that. He wasn't going to tell her where they were bound. At times she wondered if even Harry had decided what their destination was. He'd told the last rental clerk, this time a man, that they were headed for Boston. He'd even bought maps of the Eastern Seaboard. Then he'd headed west again.

There was a pay phone at the convenience store where he stopped for gas. To save time, Valentina handled the pump while Harry called Washington.

"Something really strange has happened," he said when he returned. "My cousin Sikina showed up."

"Your family is growing. It used to consist of just a set of parents in Elko. Now you've added a host of other relatives," Valentina said.

Harry frowned. "It wouldn't be bad if they weren't so troublesome. Sikina is Badr's wife." He started the car again and headed back toward the Interstate.

"And she's in Washington? Shouldn't she be at his bedside, holding his hand?"

"Apparently not. Konig says she waltzed into the police station hoping to find me. She claims, according to him, that Badr sent her to seek my protection."

Valentina considered that idea. "Actually, I've found it is rather dangerous to be around you, Harry. But that does mean that Badr doesn't realize someone thinks you know something about his secret. About the treasure."

"True," he mused. "It doesn't sound right though, Val. Badr isn't what you'd call a besotted and caring husband. He considers Sikina a necessary evil, just another possession."

"But wouldn't he ..."

Harry stopped at a light. He drummed his fingers against the steering wheel. "That's the problem. He wouldn't care what happened to her. Their's has not been a marriage made in paradise. He was considering returning her to her family. Since her father is dead, that means to Dad and me. We're the closest male relatives."

"Return her? Like an empty container for recycling?"

"Just about." The light changed and Harry followed a line of traffic up onto the highway once more. He chuckled softly. "He should have known what Sikina was like. When we were kids, she and her sister Fatima followed us around each summer. He thought them pests then, especially Sikina with her constant questions. Once he even took her back to her father and gave instructions on the proper way to train women. Badr wanted a subservient wife, not one who thought."

Valentina chewed her lip, considering what he'd said, then slurped the last bit of her vanilla shake. "What if that's why she's in Washington? What if Badr was trying to get rid of her just because the opportunity existed?"

"Why to the States? Dad's closer. He's in Cairo, not thousands of air miles away. Besides, when Badr broached the idea to me a few months ago, I laughed at him. Told him to get his head out of the archives and remember which century he lived in. As far as I was concerned, if he wanted to divorce Sikina it was fine. But he had to see to her support until she found another husband."

"What did he say?"

"That she wouldn't look for another husband if he was paying for her keep."

Valentina sighed. "Sounds like a real prick to me."

Harry laughed at that. "I'm sure Sikina would agree with you. She lived in the States for a while and hasn't been able to accept all the old ways, ways that Badr is determined to keep."

"Hmm. Doesn't get us any closer to a solution, does it?"

"Nope. How are you feeling now?"

"Fine. Thinking ahead to dinner, really. I think I'd like to try normal food. Something simple," Valentina said. "Like a steak." She reclined her seat a bit and stared at the ceiling. "With baked potato, sour cream, and butter."

"Think you can handle it?" Harry changed lanes to zip around a slower moving semi.

Picturing the meal, especially now that she was no longer feeling guilty about deviating from Todd's rules, Valentina grinned. "Oh, yeah. I'm looking forward to it."

"Steak it is then. Still sleepy?"

"Not really. Tell me more about life in Yemen when you were a kid. What kind of games did you play? I'm guessing it wasn't baseball."

The sign welcoming them to Illinois flashed by. Harry glanced at the clock on the dashboard. At least it was Sunday. When they hit St. Louis there wouldn't be any rush-hour traffic. They'd stop for dinner there at any rate. If Valentina wanted steak, he'd take her to the best restaurant St. Louis had to offer. It would be a big improvement over all the forty-nine cent casino breakfast specials they'd eaten in the old days, staying up late to get the best deal.

"Not baseball," he agreed. "We stayed with Badr's family. They had a house in Sirwah which was closer to the excavation sites at Marib than San'a'. Plus the house was a lot more comfortable than a tent. Yemen is mountainous so the residents have built multi-storied houses rather than follow the Bedouin way of life. The climate is cooler as well."

"Does that mean you didn't tend camels?"

Harry chuckled. "No camels. At least not at our house. But that's not surprising when you remember that we were an academic household. We kids were left pretty much on our own to roam the hills. We invented games, basing nearly all of them on the stories we heard at night, or on an imitation of what our fathers did during the day. Any broken utensil could become an artifact in our eyes. And even pesky girls like Fatima and Sikina could be the prey of evil *efreets*.

"We played with them most frequently because they were the only other children who didn't have household errands to keep them busy all day. Badr was irritated by their presence more often than not. He was already too serious then. He didn't even think my treasure was worth hiding."

Valentina sat up straight abruptly. Her green eyes glowed with excitement. "Harry!" She breathed his name just as she had long ago. "The treasure! Could it be the same?"

He had jumped to the same conclusion. Harry pulled off to the side of the road, putting the car in park, letting the engine idle. He let the rest of the traffic whip past them.

"I don't know, Val. But what other treasure is there?" He fished in the back pocket of his jeans for his wallet.

Valentina watched as he flipped through the plastic sections. His driver's license, some credit cards, a photo of a pretty blond woman and an older man in a cowboy hat (the Nevada branch of his family), and a picture she had forgotten. Even though she'd just gotten a brief glimpse of it, Valentina knew it showed Harry and herself. It had been taken at the Mount Charleston Lodge. The mountain was just an hour's drive from Las Vegas. A group of students had gone there on Christmas Day to play in the snow. It hadn't been deep, but it had been enough to make the day special. Denny Northrup, Harry's best friend, had brought along bottles of champagne to toast the day. In the picture she and Harry were preparing to drink from the same glass.

It wasn't a photograph Harry was searching for, though. He pulled a yellowed piece of paper from the last compartment and tossed it into Valentina's lap. "Look at that."

The paper was brittle. The edges crumbled in her hands.

"The Treasure of the Unifier," Harry said quietly.

It was a map. Dark lines wavered to denote a labyrinth of streets. Buildings were single squares. In the corner of one of them there was a large black X.

"A treasure map!" Valentina cried. She threw her arms around Harry's neck and kissed him quickly in delight.

She tasted of Tic Tacs, and vanilla ice cream. Of the nectar of Eden.

Valentina was just as surpised at her actions as Harry was pleased. "Harry?" she murmured. She gazed into his eyes, her lips still parted, and warm from contact with his.

"Val." He touched the caramel wisps of her hair. Brushed them back tenderly.

"Oh, Harry," she said and melted against him.

The map lay forgotten between them. He kissed her, savoring the moment. All too soon she'd remember the man back in Washington, the one who'd bought her a diamond rather than explain its crystal structure.

"I knew you'd remember," Valentina said, a bit breathlessly, when they parted. She turned her attention back to the scrap of paper, smoothing it out on her lap.

If she didn't want to talk about that sudden sweet kiss, then Harry decided he wasn't ready to discuss the lapse either. "It isn't a treasure really," he explained. "Or it didn't used to be. Badr and I found this secret compartment. Just a hole behind some loose stonework inside the house. There were some old papers inside it. The writing had already faded by then. Badr wanted to study it. I just saw the spot as a perfect place to keep my catcher's mitt and baseball. For posterity's sake, I left my best baseball cards there as well. Hell, they're probably worth a few bucks now. But certainly no treasure worth killing over."

"But do the people who are trying to kill you and Badr know that?"

"Obviously not. But I don't think the cards, mitt, and ball are there anymore, Val," Harry said.

She nodded. "Absolutely. Badr has put something there for safekeeping."

"Something that is worth killing for." Harry put the car back into gear and watched for a chance to pull back out into the steady flow of traffic. "I think it's time to try to get in touch with Badr," he said.

Chapter Seven

COLE RUSKIN TAPPED lightly on the door. He'd never had the occasion to visit a room in such a posh hotel before. The subtle gray and mauve colors of the wallpaper and carpet were attractive, but a little washed out for his taste. Crystal chandeliers had always seemed a little busy to him, all those glinting pieces constantly turning to catch and reflect the light. He supposed he just lacked the class to appreciate the décor.

He was quite qualified to appreciate a high-class woman though. When Sikina Hashid opened the door and gave him that slow, sensual smile, Ruskin felt the burning start in the pit of his stomach. It didn't matter that he knew there was no chance of living out the fantasies he'd had about her since her visit to his office earlier in the day. As long as he had a reason to visit her, he continued to dream.

"Cole," she cooed in that soft, exotic voice. "You have news for me?"

He inhaled deeply as he passed her, breathing in the tantalizing scent of hibiscus blossoms. "Smith called in," he said.

She waved him to a seat on a plush silver-toned sofa. The rug was a deeper rose than the one in the hall, but the same color scheme was carried out in the suite. At least there was no crystal dangling from the ceiling. The lamps gave off a soft muted glow that complimented Sikina's skin. She wore a long cream-silk robe and her long blue-black hair was down, falling nearly to her waist.

When she curled upon the sofa with him, the robe fell apart to display streamline legs. He was sure she didn't have a stitch on beneath the silk.

Sikina poured him a glass of wine. "Tell me," she urged. "Where is Hadi hiding? I would like to make arrangements to join him as soon as possible."

Ruskin accepted the goblet and sipped at the heady vintage. He'd been off duty for the last hour. He'd grabbed a beer and a burger before working up his courage to come to Sikina's hotel. He wasn't sure what Konig would say of this visit. Or about the fact that he intended to tell Sikina Hashid where Smith finally came to nest.

The drapes were pulled back. Because the suite was on one of the upper floors of the high-rise, the view of Washington at night was magical. He identified the Washington Monument, the Dome of the Capital, and other sights from the pattern of spotlights. The aura of the city had a fascination that lured many guests to their windows. But he wasn't a paying guest here, nor could Washington hold a candle to the lush woman next to him.

"Well, there's a problem in your joining your cousin," Ruskin said slowly.

Her dark eyes widened in puzzlement.

"He's still on the run. He called in from Indiana, but he was moving on from there."

"Indiana." She lingered on the word thoughtfully. Sattam's inquiries had elicited a different direction. Obviously Hadi had lied to the woman at the airport. Charlotte, North Carolina had not been his intended destination. "That is in your Midwest, is it not? Where in Indiana was he when he called?"

Ruskin took another sip of wine, more of a gulp. He tried to keep his eyes on the view from the window. But they kept straying to the woman, and that sensual display of warm flesh. "Terre Haute. It's on the border of Illinois. Could be he's heading for Chicago."

When he had left, she would check a map, but Sikina doubted that Hadi would be turning north toward the Great Lakes. If she guessed right, he was being as single minded as a bee returning to its hive. "So far," she murmured softly. "And yet, it is not so far, is it? Is Hadi not flying to his destination? He is making inconvenient stops, is he not?"

"He's driving."

She had known that, but perhaps this besotted fool would give her more information if she continued to play the helpless dove. "I do not understand. This country is large. It takes days to travel in an automobile."

Ruskin stared into his glass a moment then quickly finished the wine off. "I think he wants time," he said. "You see, he's not alone."

"One of your brave men is with him? To protect him?"

Ruskin smiled. He really wasn't unattractive when he did so, Sikina decided. "No, a young woman. Someone he used to know."

"Is she beautiful?"

"Compared to you? No."

She rewarded him with a wide grin and moved closer to him on the sofa. "You think I am beautiful?"

A warm flush colored his face. "Very," Ruskin said. "I'm sure your husband thinks so, too."

"He does not admire me." Sikina let her bottom lip quiver slightly. "He is dying. Soon I will be alone."

Ruskin shifted uncomfortably in his seat. "Sikina, I'm sure that ..."

"Say it again," she pleaded. "I like the way you say my name."

He swallowed once. "Sikina," he said.

She moved into his arms. "Hold me, Cole. Keep me safe."

"I can't ..."

"Tonight," she purred. "Tonight you will keep me safe. Love me just a little. Then you will tell me about my cousin Hadi?"

Ruskin's arms closed tightly around her, drawing her nearer. He breathed deeply of her scent, ran a large hand along the elegant curve of her spine. "Yes," he murmured. "The next time Smith calls, I will tell you where to find him," he promised.

When the sun rose on the second day of their being on the run, Valentina found Harry had pulled off the Interstate and parked along side the road. The signpost claimed they were thirty miles outside of Kansas City.

Harry was already awake and counting the cash in his wallet. He didn't even look up when she yawned and stretched in her seat. He fingered his MasterCard.

"Morning, gorgeous. Sleep well?" He didn't wait for an answer.

"How much cash have you got with you?"

Valentina bent to rummage in her purse. "Twenty ... twenty-four bucks. Handful of change, mostly pennies."

Harry sighed and leaned his head back against the seat. "Looks like we linger a bit then. I've got about forty. Probably not enough to place a transatlantic call at a pay phone plus eat today. We'll have to let Konig check on Badr. I just hope my plastic is still in good shape. After a year away, I don't know what the credit line is on it. In any case, I think a stop at a bank is in order."

"Maybe we can find a mall," Valentina suggested. "I'd like to burn my present clothes if at all possible." She waved a J.C. Penney credit card at him. "I'll even splurge and get you something."

Harry tossed his wallet into her lap and started the car. "In return then, I promise you we'll sleep in a bed tonight."

"You say the nicest things. Where will we be by then?"

"Hopefully, Denver."

"I thought so," Valentina said. She was silent a moment then she turned on him. "You damn fool!" she stormed. "You're headed straight to Vegas, aren't you?"

Harry didn't confess. "Why do you think that, Val?"

"Don't give me that innocent look. We haven't gotten off Interstate 70 yet."

"It doesn't go to Las Vegas," he pointed out.

"No, it dumps us in Utah. You hate Utah."

"It has some great ski runs."

Valentina wasn't to be put off. "You don't ski," she pointed out.

"It's been five years, Val. How do you know I haven't learned?"

"Give me a reason why you would have," she insisted.

Harry thought for a moment. "Snow bunnies."

Valentina snorted. "Brainless twerps," she declared, dismissing the idea. "You didn't really learn to ski, did you?"

He stared ahead. He hadn't returned to the freeway, but had driven down the country road. "Does Todd ski?" he asked.

Her answer was slow in coming. "Yes," she admitted reluctantly. "But ..."

"Then I hate skiing," Harry said. "I hope he breaks his leg."

Valentina was surprised to find she echoed the wish. What was wrong with her? She had promised to marry Todd McAllister!

They'd set the date. Her dress had been ordered. The caterers had been contracted.

She twisted the diamond ring on her hand. "Let's not talk about Todd," she said.

"Which equates to the same thing as let's not talk about us either." He sounded angry. Hurt.

"There hasn't been any *us* for a long time, Harry."

"Until yesterday, Val."

His voice was quiet now, as if he were mentally replaying that impulsive kiss. Kisses, she corrected. They hadn't been far from her mind since then either.

"I want you back," he said.

Valentina stared at the ring on her hand as if it were a talisman. A beam of sunlight struck the faceted surface creating colorful rainbow prisms. It was a symbol of her promise to another man. It was just a mineral formation, a creation of heat and pressure within Mother Earth.

"Five years is a long time," she said. "People change."

"Have you, Val?"

Had she? Valentina pondered the question. She had put the past behind her. She had renounced archaeology and become a Washington secretary. She'd met Todd when she interviewed for a position in his office. He hadn't given her the job. He'd asked her out instead, explaining that his principles wouldn't allow him to date an employee. She hadn't minded losing the promotion that being his secretary would have been. There would be other offices, other chances.

What had it been about Todd that had impressed her? His winning smile? It had gotten him votes back in Minnesota. His dependability? In the six months she'd known him, he'd always been on time, had always acted as expected. He followed all the rules, knew all the right people. And he'd groomed her to be the perfect mate. Todd had guided her choice of clothing, the change in her hair style, the places she went, the people she met, the food she ate. And because she was lonely, she had let him.

Five years had been a long time.

"I waited for you to come after me," she said softly. "When you didn't, I knew I had to change. I couldn't be the same girl I had been. Part of me died."

Harry continued to stare ahead at the road. "I know the feeling. If we'd just talked it out, Val ..."

Valentina laughed derisively. "Harry, we never talked."

He kept his attention on the broken line down the middle of the narrow pavement. "I still don't want to *just* talk with you," he growled and turned his head briefly to glare at her. "This isn't the easiest drive. And I'm not talking about the distance."

The sensation that she had butterflies in her stomach had surfaced days ago, when he'd come striding across the museum in her grandmother's wake. It had been growing daily, but now the beasts were in full flight. Todd had never looked at her with such undisguised desire. Harry's blue eyes looked almost turbulent. They swept over her quickly then swung back to the road. His hands on the wheel tightened.

Valentina fought down the breathless feeling. Five years. Five incredibly long years.

He was back in control quickly. "There it is. I thought I remembered seeing a sign for this exit."

Up ahead, Valentina could see a square building. She didn't even have to read the lettering to know it was a convenience store. They all seemed to be built on a single plan.

Harry pulled the Corolla up to the gasoline pumps and turned off the engine. "Can you manage a fast breakfast here, honey?"

Since she had succesfully kept down the steak and baked potato the night before, Valentina felt she was ready for anything.

Harry rubbed at his front teeth. "See if they've got toothbrushes, would you?"

A toothbrush! She had never heard a sweeter word. Valentina pulled open the car door and rushed into the store.

She found not only toothbrushes, but mouthwash and bars of soap. While Harry filled the gas tank, Valentina asked the clerk if there were public restrooms, explaining they'd been driving all night and needed to freshen up. She had the keys to both the men's and women's when he came through the door.

They both had clean shirts to wear, thanks to a gift shop near the restaurant where they'd eaten the night before. Valentina hugged hers, a fresh bar of soap, and her new toothbrush to her chest and locked the restroom door behind her. She filled the wash basin with warm water and stripped. The smooth satiny feel of soap against her skin was akin to heaven. Her discarded T-shirt served as a towel.

It felt wonderful to be clean once more, even if she was still wearing nearly the same clothes she'd put on Saturday morning. Only the shirt had changed. Now it was powder blue and emblazoned with the outline of the state of Missouri. Mentally, Valentina made a list of things to purchase when they found a mall. Jeans, shorts, light-weight blouses, lingerie ... The list could be endless the way she was feeling. And none of it would be acceptable to Todd McAllister. At the thought, she grinned at her reflection in the mirror over the basin. The rebellion was full-blown. She'd given up his diet, and now the conservative neutral-colored clothing he preferred would bite the dust. The jeans she wore to clean house would no longer be orphans.

The restroom was little more than a closet. The bottom half of the window had been slapped with white paint in an effort to afford some privacy. To open it, however, the sash was drawn upward, so the painted section was really an afterthought. Valentina wondered how often the window was opened. Maybe when they cleaned the room. A faint aroma of disinfectant clung to the air. A short partition separated the toilet from the sink and window. Valentina ducked behind it to balance on the commode while she tied up her shoes once more.

The sound didn't register at first. Then she recognized it. Someone was pushing the window open. From the outside!

Valentina glanced at the door. It was next to the window and opened toward her. The simple bolt was still thrown, locking her inside.

The sash squealed a bit. It hadn't been oiled recently. She could hear the heavy breathing of the person outside. Valentina stood and peeked carefully over the top of the partition, then ducked back into hiding quickly. Her breath came in quick gasps. Her mind raced.

The man at the window hadn't seen her. He'd been turned away, trying to push himself up and into the room. His plaid shirt wasn't clean. He had thinning, gray hair, and a scrawny neck. As she listened, he managed to get a grip on the window sill.

He didn't know she was there. Surely, he didn't! He was making too much noise to convince her that stealth was involved. Did he intend to hide in the room waiting for the next woman to come in? For that matter, where could he hide? The partition shielded half the room from view through the window, but wasn't a blind from the door.

Valentina looked for a weapon. The paper towel dispenser was tightly bolted to the wall. She didn't have a large purse loaded down with trivial but necessary junk. What she wouldn't have given for a backpack loaded with books! That would put a dent in anyone's head. But the only moveable object in the room seemed to be the plastic trash receptacle. It would probably bounce if she hit him with it.

Beggars couldn't be overly fastidious though. Valentina reached for the trash can with her left hand. In her right she hefted the still slick bar of Ivory.

The man huffed and puffed and fell into the room, head first. In a flash, Valentina stepped from hiding and hurled the soap. It connected nicely, striking squarely in the center of the man's forehead as he looked up in shock.

"Haaarrrryyyyy!" Valentina screamed at the top of her lungs. A banshee couldn't have sounded more terrifying to the downed invader. His legs were still crumpled against the wall, his toes draped over the window ledge.

"Harry!" she shrilled again then smashed the trash can over the stunned man's head. Discarded paper towels flew into the air then floated down over the intruder. "You pervert!" Valentina hit him again. The plastic container did indeed bounce.

Someone tried the door handle. Then something heavy smashed against the door. The wood groaned, but held.

The man on the floor tried to grab at Valentina's shoe. She kicked at him and bounced the can off him again.

The door was struck again. Hard. This time the latch gave and Harry barrelled into the room. He tripped on the sprawled man on the floor and caught himself against the edge of the sink. "Val! Honey, are you all right?" he gasped.

"Oh, Harry!" she breathed and threw herself into his arms. The trash can landed on the still-stunned victim, covering his balding head.

The store clerk stuck his head through the open door. "Jesus H. Christ!" he moaned and bent to uncover the man on the floor. "Titus, what the hell are you doing here?" he demanded, righting the trash can. He started refilling it with the scattered towels. "I told ya before, check with me before you go sleep it off!"

"You know this creep?" Harry growled, his arms still tight around Valentina's quivering form. Her head was buried against his chest. He hugged her close.

"Yeah," the clerk said and sighed. "My uncle. He comes here to hide from my aunt when he's had too much to drink. I'm sorry if he scared you, miss."

The man on the floor blinked. He'd finally fallen the rest of the way into the room. He sat up and rubbed his head. "Tried to kill me," he mumbled.

"Sure, Titus. Get on home, will you?" the store clerk urged, dragging the man to his feet and out the door.

Harry turned his attention to the girl in his arms. She was still shaking. His cheek rested against her caramel-colored locks. The scent of Ivory soap rose from her freshly scrubbed skin. "Val, honey? Are you okay?" he asked softly.

She nodded against him. She hiccupped once, then moved a scant six inches away. Her green eyes watered as she met his concerned blue ones. Tears spilled over and down her cheeks. But she wasn't crying. She was laughing.

"Oh, Harry!" Valentina giggled. "I did try to kill him. With a trash can!"

Harry ran his hand up her spine and back down in a soothing gesture. He smiled down into her upturned face. "You're a dangerous woman, Valentina Crosby. I've known that for a long time." He brushed at her tears, his touch tender.

The butterflies took over. "Oh, Harry," she murmured, her eyes shimmering with something more than just tears. "You came to rescue me."

His dark hair was wet and curling. A drop fell on her upraised face. His chest was bare and damp as well. Her new T-shirt was splotched with water from close contact with him. She could feel the quick pounding of his heart against her breast. Or was it her own heart?

Valentina gave in. Linking her hands behind Harry's neck, she raised on tip toe and kissed him. Not as she had the day before, but as she had so often five long years ago, giving herself up to the wonderful sensations of his touch, of his lips.

Far away to the east in Washington, D.C., Todd McAllister didn't even realize his wedding had just been cancelled.

Harry grinned down into Valentina's upturned face, unaware that she'd made a decision that concerned him. "Well, if that was a thank you," he said, "I'll try to be around often when you need rescuing. Although, actually, honey, you whipped the guy single-handed."

Valentina's lips were still warm from the kiss. Her legs felt slightly weak. She'd never reacted this way with Todd. But that was a moot point now. She had no intention of going back to him, or to Washington. She wasn't sure what she was going to do, or even if she wanted Harry to be a part of her life. First she had to decide what it was she wanted. For so long she'd just been measuring happiness against what she didn't want. It hadn't been enough.

As much as she hated to admit it, her grandmother had been right about Todd McAllister. He wasn't the right man for her. But was Harry Smith? She had thought so once but five years made a big difference. She wasn't the same trusting girl she'd once been. And Harry? How had the years treated him?

Valentina smiled softly at him. "Didn't you promise me breakfast?" she asked.

The T-shirt she'd bought him in St. Louis was tighter than his other shirts had been. Or perhaps she was just more aware of him, of the way the cotton pulled across his shoulders and hugged his chest.

Harry rubbed his right arm, flexing the bruised muscles. It had been a fairly sturdy door he'd thudded against earlier, Valentina admitted. Maybe she'd offer to massage it later. Maybe she wouldn't.

Valentina stood behind him at the cashier's window at the bank in Kansas City. The clerk was on the phone, checking the credit line on Harry's MasterCard. She wished she could contribute more but Todd had helped choose outfits for her trousseau a few weeks ago. His taste hadn't been exactly cheap and her Visa had been maxed out in a very short time.

The diamond ring on her finger turned as she played with it. A new nervous habit. "You need me here?" she asked.

Harry leaned casually on the counter. "Need? No. Want? Yes."

"Want is a different subject. I'll meet you at the car."

She was halfway to the door before he nodded in agreement.

Valentina headed back down the street, the way they'd come into the city proper. She hadn't been mistaken. The shop was just where she remembered seeing it.

An obnoxious bleat announced her arrival to the man behind the counter. He smiled, overly friendly. "Morning. Buying or selling?"

"Selling, I hope. That, of course, depends on the price." Valentina glanced down into the nearest case. A variety of rings, necklaces, earrings, and watches were spread out for display. Valentina tapped the glass top over the rings. "Real?"

"Best quality," he said.

"Good as VSI?"

His oily smile widened. "Very slightly included? You either know your gems or like to show off." He glanced at the ring on her hand, at her T-shirt. "I hope you didn't steal that diamond from your mother."

Valentina slid the ring off her finger. She ignored his remark. "What would you say this was worth? Your honest opinion."

"Of course." He put a jeweler's loupe to his eye and peered at the stone, turning it slightly to the left, then the right. He named a price.

"Not even close," Valentina said. She held out her hand for the ring.

The man frowned, studied the diamond again. "Is it hot?"

"Oh, it's mine alright."

"Three hundred," he said.

Valentina shook her head. "Two thousand."

He knew she was bluffing. "Five hundred," he countered.

Harry was already in the car when Valentina joined him. "How'd you make out?" she asked, dropping into the passenger's seat.

"Better than I thought. The plastic will even run to a shopping spree for you."

"I have a long list," she warned.

"No problem." He started the car and pulled back into traffic. "I got directions to the nearest shopping mall so you would stop nagging."

Valentina grinned happily and clutched her purse tighter. "So thoughtful. But I can't let you keep picking up the bill for everything, Harry. After all, I'm on the lam, too."

He glanced over at her. "Now, why do I smell a rat?"

"You're a suspicious SOB, that's why," Valentina announced. "It's part of our charm."

"What have you been up to, Val?"

"Me?"

He wasn't deceived by the innocence act. "Val."

With a superior smile, she opened her purse and took out a stack of money. "I insisted on small bills so we wouldn't have trouble spending it," she said.

Harry stopped so quickly, he screeched the tires.

"I tried to get more," Valentina continued, "but I've never been a good bargainer. A thousand ought to help though."

When the traffic behind them starting honking, Harry put the car back in gear, and turned into a parking lot. "What the hell did you sell? Your soul?" he demanded.

He could have looked happier. Instead he scowled at her.

"Don't be ridiculous. We couldn't go on indefinitely with less than sixty dollars and one credit card," Valentina insisted. "I just used what I had." She wiggled the fingers of her left hand at him. "I pawned the diamond, naturally. When this is all over I'll get it out of hock. Todd probably wouldn't like the idea of a stranger wearing it anyway."

Harry's glare didn't soften. "So you went off without asking my opinion."

"I didn't need your opinion," she said. "It was my ring, my decision."

"If you think I'm going to touch a cent of it ... Jesus, Val!"

Her eyes narrowed. Don't you swear at me, Harry Smith. This isn't exactly blood money. We need it."

"We don't."

"Do."

He sighed deeply. "Lord, and your grandmother told me you'd changed. You're still as bullheaded as you ever were."

Valentina put the money back in her purse, a smug little smile curving her lips. "That's why you love me," she said.

Harry growled deep in his throat, frustrated. The hell of it was, he thought, she was right. Too damn right.

Chapter Eight

THE SCRAWNY MAN weaved slightly when they hustled him out of the vehicle. His filthy Bedouin robes moved in the mountain breeze. His eye was already swollen where the man named after the Prophet had struck him. The bruises on the rest of his body didn't show, they only slowed his already ambling movements.

Faraday slammed the door of the jeep. The sound echoed his fury. Finding the man Nahar had not been as easy as he had thought. It had taken Mohammad the best part of a day to scour the city in his search for the thief. When he had been located, he had been in a ghat-induced stupor. A few well-placed blows had finally stirred the man's memory.

Mohammad had worn native clothing, wide flowing trousers, robe and headdress. The wicked-looking dagger thrust in his wide belt would be put to good use after Nahar Aflaq showed them the location of the treasure.

Faraday himself was the embodiment of the complete adventurer in khaki-colored denim pants, a similarly toned short-sleeved shirt and a pith helmet. He took the helmet off briefly to mop his heat-reddened face. The mountain offered little respite from the sun, but the soft breeze rolling off the heights was welcome. He turned into it, allowing it to ruffle his bright red hair. Once the treasure was his, he would kiss this Godforsaken land goodbye. He'd heard some of his fellow castaways describe the Arabian landscape as beautiful. They went on about the history of the peninsula, trotting out the Sumerians, Babylonians, Hittites, and the Israelites. They babbled about spice caravans, about caliphs, about culture. They praised the ancient cities, ogling the architecture and the busy designs that decorated building after building. They took excursions into the desert to play at being National Geographic reporters studying the life of the Bedouin. They climbed into the mountains, waded on the beaches. They found wonders where he saw a geographical prison.

Ah, but once he had the treasure that would all change.

Faraday replaced his helmet and got down to business. "Where now, thief?"

Nahar's shrunken face made his beak of a nose more prominent. He turned it, as if sniffing the air for a clue to his direction. One eye was swollen nearly shut. Perhaps he should have told Mohammad to remove his ring before striking the man, Faraday thought, then dismissed the idea. It had cut deeply at the corner of the thief's eye, but it had not loosened his tongue. It had taken a good number of blows to accomplish that.

"There," Nahar said and pointed a boney, stained finger up the mountain.

Mohammad gave him a push. "Show us," he snapped.

The dullness in the thief's good eye made Faraday wonder if the man even knew where he was; what was requested of him. He stared up the mountainside, at the rocky terrain and steep cliffs. "How far up is this queen's tomb?" Faraday demanded. "You're sure this is the correct location?"

Nahar nodded. "As if it were my own home, *efendi.*"

The information didn't cheer Faraday. He doubted if the man even had a home. They had found him hunched over in the doorway of a closed shop.

The wiry little beggar moved ahead of them, beginning the climb before Mohammad could prod him again. At first the going was not difficult. Faraday trailed behind, noting features that would guide him back once the thief had been disposed of.

He paused once and turned to look back, to get his bearings. The valley spread out far below. Sections of it were cultivated, the waving grain looking almost incongruous. He could see the ruins of some ancient building. Portions of it were completely gone. If one looked carefully, one could find strikingly similar building materials used in the construction of homes in the village. He had no interest in these remnants of history, though; only in their value in the marketplace. There was no fortune to be made in building blocks. But in the hoards of ancient monarchs, there lay a very comfortable future for him.

Mohammad and the thief were quite a distance ahead. They had worked their way out along a narrow ledge. Faraday shuddered at the thought of traversing it. He wondered if there was another way to the tomb. Since Nahar knew only a single route, that was the one he had taken. Faraday considered the slope, still watching the two men. Then, suddenly, the wiry little thief disappeared.

Faraday started forward in surprise then stayed where he was when Mohammad signaled. They had found the tomb. Within moments the thief had emerged from an opening that was hidden from Faraday's sight. In his hand was something that glinted in the afternoon sun.

From where he watched, the object looked like a jar, gracefully shaped and, he thought, crafted of gold. The warm glow it cast was like a reflection of the sun itself. It flashed in the light as if studded with jewels.

Mohammad had it in his hands now, turning it, studying it with a greed that rivaled Faraday's own. He would be wise to watch his assistant. The stocky, muscular man was just as capable of driving that wicked knife between Faraday's own ribs as he was of dispatching the thief.

Nahar said something and tried to take the artifact back. Mohammad growled an answer, pulling the jar from the thief's anxious hands. Did Nahar think the prize was his to keep, Faraday wondered? Foolish. Now that they knew the location of the treasure there was no reason to keep the man alive. Mohammad would humor him, then sink the deadly dagger into his back when he turned. No one would find the thief's body here on the desolate side of the mountain.

High above him on the ledge, the two men struggled, each trying to gain possession of the golden artifact. Nahar stepped back, his foot finding the ledge with the surety of a mountain goat.

Mohammad followed, stepped on loose rubble, and pitched sideways. His right hand still clutched the curved handle of the jar. His left waved frantically, searching for a handhold. But there was none.

Faraday watched in stunned silence as his henchman tumbled off the mountainside. The thief, Nahar, still cradling the sides of the jar between his hands, spilled with him, down into the bowels of the steeply sloping crevasse.

They were gone, with only the echo of their cries hanging in the suddenly still air. Faraday rushed to the edge, staring far down the mountain. He could see the white of Mohammad's robe. It fluttered as the wind picked up again. There was no movement other than that of the cloth. There was no sign of the filthy dark robes of Nahar, the thief. There was no glitter of gold from the sample of the treasure in the queen's tomb.

Faraday sat back and stared up at the mountain. His heart was pounding. Sweat, which had nothing to do with the air temperature or the heat rising from the rocks, beaded his brow and soaked his clothing. If he had followed them to the entrance, he thought frantically, would he, too, have ended up dead at the bottom of the cliff?

He took deep breaths, waiting for the fear to recede. Both Mohammad and Nahar died because they'd been foolish. With the wealth of an ancient empire within reach, they fought over possession of a single jar. He would not be that stupid. What did one piece matter when there was much more?

If, indeed, Badr al-Hashid had secreted a sample of the find elsewhere, then let Sikina follow her map to it. She was welcome to that small bit of treasure. He would have the lion's share. By the time she returned, the artifacts would already have been sold to the unscrupulous men who ran the very profitable illegal antiquities trade. And he would already be gone.

Faraday got to his feet and climbed the rest of the way to the tomb. Carefully, he inched along the narrow ledge, avoiding the rubble, ensuring himself of sturdy handholds among the jutting rocks and scrub brush. When he thought he had reached the location he stopped. There was no opening visible, but he felt sure it would be carefully disguised. He avoided looking down. He had no desire to be reminded of what happened to those who let greed get the best of them here on the mountain.

Slowly he inched along, his fingers as well as eyes searching the area. He tested each rock, looked behind each bush, using the sensitivity of his surgeon's hands. Soon they were torn and bleeding, but he searched on. Farther and farther, he worked the length of the ledge and then back, rechecking every crevice, every shadow.

The tomb had disappeared.

Chapter Nine

HARRY HUNG THE phone back on its hook and stood staring at it in bewilderment. "I don't understand it," he muttered.

"Understand what?" Valentina took another bite of the hot dog she'd bought before leaving the shopping mall. She felt like a new woman. The red, yellow, and white pattern on her new shorts outfit was as vibrant as her feelings. She'd replaced her high tops with bright red canvas espadrilles. She knew the new outfit complimented her looks from the way Harry had looked at her when she'd skipped from the store, a number of plastic bags swinging on her arm. Of course, that hungry stare could have been for the long expanse of bare leg. She hadn't forgotten what drove him a bit crazy. The fact that his gaze still often dropped to her legs pleased her immensely.

Harry took the hot dog from her and helped himself to a substantial bite, then led the way back to the car. He'd been much more conservative in his purchases. A few pairs of jeans, some long-sleeved shirts, and various essentials had been the extent of his spree. He'd added two backpacks, but Valentina's purchases overflowed hers. He didn't like to imagine what the total of her purchases had been. At least she'd been fast. They were ready to get back on the road in just an hour. Only the call to Washington delayed them.

"Konig says that Badr has disappeared from the hospital."

"Gosh! You don't think he's been kidnapped, do you?"

She had a dab of mustard at the corner of her mouth. Harry

resisted the temptation to kiss it away. "They doubt it." He held the passenger door open for her. His eyes lingered on her newly exposed legs as she swung them inside the car. This trip was getting more difficult all the time. He'd be lucky if he could keep his mind on sorting out the mystery of Badr's secret find and how he himself was involved in it. Rather than getting easier, the problem seemed to be getting more tangled.

Once they were back on the Interstate and past the entrance toll booth of the Kansas Turnpike, Valentina pulled the tattered piece of map from the glove compartment.

"We're agreed, aren't we, that Badr has put some kind of artifact in the old hiding place?" she asked. "And you think it might be linked to this ancient queen, right?"

"Bilqis, the Queen of Saba. It's only a shot in the dark, Val. Though the more I think about it, the more I'm convinced that's the only find Badr would go to so much trouble over. He lives in San'a' and the cache on that map is in Sirwah. That means he made a special trip to get the artifact out of the city."

Valentina fingered the scrap of yellowing paper. "Do you think the men who tried to kill you knew about the existence of the map?"

Harry's expression was grim. "They made no mention of it when they forced their way into your grandmother's house."

"If they thought you knew where Badr had hidden this treasure, how were they to get the information if you were dead, Harry? They had to know about the map."

"A map drawn by a couple of kids? Why would anyone think I'd still be carrying it?"

Valentina's finger followed the snaking lines of the streets and the lopsided squares that represented houses. Did it look like a creation of children? Or did it have the appearance of a reminder hastily scratched?

"Why did you still have it with you?" she asked.

Harry drummed his fingers against the wheel. The needle of the speedometer crept to seventy, but he didn't notice. Keeping to the left lane he whipped past the other traffic.

"Sentimental, I guess," he said.

Valentina thought about the photograph he still carried of her. Was he sentimental? Or just clinging to memories of better times?

"The map reminded me of the adventures I'd had in Yemen," Harry continued. "I always had good stories to write in those essays we did the first week of school. You know, the ones about 'what I did on my vacation.' I didn't think Badr still had his half." He glanced over at Valentina briefly. "Maybe we're wrong about this. If the other piece of the map was tossed out long ago, no one would even know about this section of it. And in that case, why would the Treasure of the Unifier be part of this mess?"

"It does sound far-fetched. But that's only because we know the map was a prop in a kid's game. Even if Badr didn't have his part of it any more, he still knew where the hiding place was. Could still use it."

"Yeah." Harry glared ahead. The exit for Lawrence, Kansas, whipped by. "So the question we have to ask ourselves is whether the map is involved at all."

Valentina nodded. "Who else knows about it? Anyone other than you and Badr? Were there other boys involved in that particular game?"

He shook his head. "Nope. There were rarely any other kids to join in. They all had chores to keep them busy. In some cases, they were helping support their family. Not exactly a *Leave It To Beaver* neighborhood." He paused, still thinking back in time.

"Sikina," he said.

"Beg your pardon?"

"Sikina, Badr's wife. She and her sister, Fatima, were there that summer." He frowned, trying to verify the memory. "I'm sure of it."

"But you said Konig told you she was in Washington," Valentina protested. "That she inquired after you the day after we left."

"That doesn't mean she wasn't in D.C. before then. Hmm." The tips of his fingers had a definite beat to them now, as they tapped nervously against the wheel.

Valentina twisted in her seat, pulling one leg up beneath her as she turned toward him. Her bare knee was close to his thigh, but Harry didn't notice.

"Surely Sikina wouldn't try to kill her own husband," Valentina insisted. "If he received acclaim for his find, even if the circumstances were suspicious, it would reflect well on her. She would profit from it."

"You're basing your thinking in the wrong culture, honey. Think back to your Anthropology 101 class. Wasn't there a section on the Middle East? Women don't marry for love there. Marriages are arranged by parents, and most often the chosen spouse is a relative. Families keep close ties."

"It still sounds too fantastic to me," Valentina said. "What about her sister? What happened to Fatima? Perhaps her husband ..."

"Nope. He's a stockbroker in New York City. Still it's a good idea to check with her," Harry said. "What kind of change have you got? We'll call from the next rest stop."

The sign for Topeka services was reached quickly. While Harry placed the call, Valentina wandered off and bought a Babe Ruth candy bar from a vending machine, then added a coke. Now that she'd put the despised diet behind her, she found she was hungry nearly all the time.

She leaned against the car. She could see the bank of pay phones from the parking lot. She also saw the calculating looks a couple of women gave Harry. He appeared to be unconscious of the attention he was drawing.

Valentina sipped her drink. Harry did look awfully good. Unlike Todd, he didn't have a spare inch of fat on him. Todd had already been fighting a battle with his waistline. The two men were about the same age. Harry was actually a year older, but he was as hard and lean as he'd been at school. She remembered the feel of his bare, damp chest under her cheek earlier that morning when he'd rushed to her rescue. Remembered the fire that had flashed in his sky-blue eyes, and the answering quickness in the pit of her stomach.

Had it been only yesterday that she'd been adamant about marrying Todd McAllister? It seemed like years, but indeed only a few hours had passed.

Harry slammed the receiver back on its hook and hurried over to the car. " 'Tima hasn't seen her sister." He yanked the door open. "It took a while to get her to stop chattering and answer questions." He grinned mischievously. His drooping mustache twitched beneath the reflected double image of Valentina on the mirrored lenses of his sunglasses. "At least I called collect," he said.

"Did she know anything about the map?"

Harry backed the car out of the parking spot. "Didn't even

remember it."

"Do you think that means Sikina has forgotten it as well?"

"Not a chance." Upon rejoining the turnpike, Harry put his foot down again. The car leapt ahead. "I think there's a link, Val. Sikina has always been jealous that her sister was allowed to marry a foreigner and stay in the States and she wasn't. Fatima claims that Sikina had an American sweetheart before she was sent back to San'a'. She couldn't remember his name, only that he was a medical student and had red hair."

Valentina sighed. "Not much help. I still don't see the connection though. Even if she remembers the map, and knows that Badr is using the hiding place for some other nefarious purpose now, why would Sikina try to kill him? Or you?"

"Me? I don't know, unless she's got some vendetta going against all her male relatives. But Badr?" Harry mused. "I can see her reasoning."

"Harry!" Valentina shouted, astonished at his complacent answer. "What's he do? Beat her?"

"He could, but I don't think Badr would care to show that much attention to Sikina. He is such a stickler for the old ways that he restricts her activities." The Corolla closed on a semi quickly. The big truck hugged the right lane, slowing for the exit. Harry glanced in his rear view mirror, then whipped the rental car around it. "How would you react, honey, if a man told you how to dress, how to act, what to eat, and with whom to associate?" he asked.

Valentina knew exactly how she would react. She just had. Todd McAllister had guided her every move, her every thought. It had taken just one little crack in that narrowly bound world for her to throw it all away. It didn't matter that she'd chosen it of her own free will. She'd been determined to find a life that didn't offer her the exhilaration she'd known with Harry. With Todd there had never been any overwhelming bursts of emotion. Things had been pat and correct. And boring.

All it had taken was a taste of forbidden food to set her off. Or had it? Hadn't she been feeling mutinous ever since she'd looked into Harry's eyes again that night on the museum patio? She'd directed that anger at Harry rather than at Todd. But it had never been Harry that she'd been furious with, it had been her straight-laced fiancé.

What had driven a chink in the foundation of Sikina's ivory

tower? Had a word, a look, driven her to contemplate murdering her husband?

Valentina still found it hard to accept. "What's Sikina like?"

"She's a knockout."

"That's not what I meant," Valentina growled.

Harry grinned back at her. "Yes, it is. You wanted to hear about her sultry, dark eyes, golden-toned skin, and ..."

"I get the picture."

"Not my type," he assured her.

"That's a backhanded insult if I every heard one. So you don't think my eyes are sultry, and my skin is ..."

"'Asal," Harry murmured, his caressing tone turning the foreign word into an endearment. "If I were a poet, I would compare your movements to the graceful sway of a date palm. Your hair would be of a texture to be compared with the finest gossamer silk. The moon would envy the alabaster-like qualities of your skin."

"Alabaster is a rock." Valentina pointed out. "But go on."

"But what a special rock, 'asal, he insisted. "White and translucent. But let's move on, shall we? I might say that the overflowing coffers of Solomon could not offer gems as perfect as your emerald eyes."

"More rocks, huh?"

"You're a tough audience."

"Don't let me interrupt you, Harry. What else would you say if you were a poet?"

He paused, considering. "Your voice is like the call of a night bird ..."

"Which night bird?"

"Nightingale?"

"Trite."

"Brush turkey? Bald eagle? Passenger pigeon?"

"What's the matter with a dove?" Valentina insisted.

Harry glanced over at her. "Now who's being trite?"

"Don't let me stop you," she urged. "What comes next?"

"Hmm. Let's see. What's left? Gazelle-like limbs?"

She tiled her hand back and forth. "Iffy. I'm still not sure about that date tree stuff. Can't you do better?"

Harry chuckled. "You sure McAllister would want you listening to a more intimate comparison? I'm trying to play it safe here, 'asal."

"'*Asal*, huh ... I'm just guessing, but that means *honey*, doesn't it? I don't think Omár Kháyyám kept his endearments that meager."

"I'm not working in iambic pentameter either. You want me to steal stuff from the Rubáiyát?"

Valentina sighed. "It would only sound right if we were surrounded by Persian rugs and scads of pillows. I suppose we really should get back to solving the mystery of why people want to kill you."

"Yeah. McAllister probably wants to save the loaf of bread and wine lines for himself anyway."

"A wedge of Brie, a nice little Chardonnay, and thou," Valentina murmured sarcastically under her breath. She would have preferred pizza and beer. She really didn't miss Todd McAllister at all.

The soft countryside with its gentle hills and lush, green forest land eased into wide, rolled out prairies the deeper they drove into Kansas.

Valentina stared out the window, watching the landscape change shape and color. What would push a woman to murder her husband? she wondered. And why was Harry so sure that Sikina was behind the attack on Badr? It had taken only a moment for him to jump from the thought to considering it a proven fact. But it wasn't.

Although Valentina realized that the culture in the Middle East was very different from that of the Western world, she still didn't see how that equated to a murder plot. Harry confidently pointed out that Sikina's upbringing was one of rampant confusion. Her impressionable years had been spent in a girls' school in New York, where she met the daughters of the elite and accepted invitations to their homes. It had been at those gatherings, according to Fatima, that Sikina had flirted with young men. It was an acceptable practice in Christian countries but not in the Islamic world. Her father had plucked her from a secular social life and plopped her back into the sequestered one praised by the Prophet Mohammad in the Koran. Harry had even run through the list of admonitions. To an American woman, especially a strong personality like Valentina's, they all seemed to boil down to one point, that it was a man's world and women should stay out of it. She seethed as he told of families rejoicing at the birth of a boy, but ignoring the birth of a girl; of women receiving a portion of their father's wealth, but men receiving two portions; of men choosing a bride without seeing her, based on the recommendations of mothers, aunts, and sisters. After seeing the freedom with which American girls chose their own mates, she could guess what Sikina's feelings had been upon being told she would marry Badr. Sikina had to bear the added insult of seeing her own sister enter the forbidden Western world by marrying an American stockbroker.

But was that enough to make Sikina want to murder her husband? They'd spent ten quiet years together, apparently content.

Valentina wished she knew more about Harry's cousins—the tragic Sikina and the driven Badr. Valentina switched gears, and turned over the equally confusing events linked to Badr. What would cause an eminent epigraphist to ignore the rules of his trade? Although an archaeological find such as Badr lusted after would thrill the academic world, without proper, careful documentation it could be challenged. He may have found, through disreputable sources, the tomb of an ancient queen, but removing artifacts from it without government sanction or the assistance of a trained team would sully the importance of the find. Surely, even in his eagerness to prove Bilqis's existence, Badr would adhere to official guidelines.

The man Harry had painted with his stories showed signs of strain. The too-serious boy, growing to manhood in the shadow of a famous father and his continued finds, had become a man bent upon professional destruction. Although it had not been proven that he had dealings with nefarious men, merely the implication that he had paid various thieves for artifacts had cast a pall over his academic career. Where once Badr had been sought out as a valued member of excavation teams, he had been passed over in recent years. It had only been through the manipulations of Dawud al-Bakil that Badr had become a member of the project upon which Harry himself had served during the past year.

Valentina tried to sort out the facts, unsubstantiated as they were. Back to the beginning then. Not the hazy conjectured events in Arabia, but the crystal clear ones in Washington, D.C.

Someone had tried to kill Harry. An unknown sniper had shot at him during the reception at the museum.

Valentina chewed her lip. How had they known that Harry would be on that patio? The outdoor areas had been closed to the guests until her own grandmother had begun playing Cupid. That meant that whoever had shot at them had been a guest at the reception, had seen that Harry was on the patio within easy range. What had they hoped to gain by his death? Harry himself may claim to believe it had been a warning, but Valentina didn't agree with that. The assassin had merely been a bad shot. If that bullet had found its target, would someone claiming to be a doctor have swept down on them and lifted Harry's wallet, and thus the map?

The map. It was still curious that a scrap of paper tied to a children's game long ago appeared to be the only link they could come up with to a treasure.

She may be confused about why anyone would want to kill Harry, and on Sikina's alleged link to the attack on Badr, but Valentina was sure the map was a valid clue. Given Badr's recent history, there was no other answer. He had hidden something of value in the secret compartment where, long ago, Harry had left an all-American treasure of baseball equipment.

Valentina pushed the uncooperative pieces of the jigsaw puzzle to the back of her mind and concentrated on the landscape. In Kansas, if anywhere, she thought, it would be easy to believe the world was indeed flat. The land was nearly level and stretched toward a distant horizon. Once buffalo had roamed here in herds that stretched from one horizon to the next. Once Texas longhorn cattle had been driven across these same vast fields, headed toward railheads in towns like Wichita and Dodge City, names that titillated the imagination with pictures of rough men and even rougher ways. Today wire fences cut the open spaces into a grid pattern of pastures. A far tamer breed of heifer grazed here now, and sought shade under the widely spaced clumps of trees that sprange up near water sources.

The Interstate wove its way through the vast landscape of farms. Signs flashed by while she pondered. Emporia, El Dorado. The road wound over a series of lakes. Forests of dead trees thrust their dark, empty branches from the water as if reaching for aid to escape the rising water. Curious, Valentina thought, letting her thoughts drift from the task of sorting out the odd collection of facts and theories. In an area where sod houses had once been built due to the lack of timber, present-day Kansans appeared to have drowned their trees. The site was mysterious and eerie. Valentina was glad they weren't passing through the area on a dismal day or at dusk.

Wichita. Valentina dozed, only half aware of the miles. She was just rousing herself, feeling slightly guilty for dropping off when Harry was taking the brunt of the driving, when a new sign loomed and was gone. Oklahoma City. "Shouldn't we see a sign for Denver instead of Oklahoma City?" Valentina asked.

"Huh?" Harry came out of his trance. He hadn't gotten any closer to solving the mystery but he was working on one helluva headache. "Oklahoma City? We shouldn't be anywhere near it. Oklahoma is south of Kansas. We're headed west."

"On I-70?" Valentina stared out the window, concentrating on the shoulder of the road. Another small sign came up and was gone as they rushed by. "I hate to tell you this, Harry, but I haven't noticed anything that says we're still on 70. All the signs say we're on Interstate 35."

The Wellington exit went by.

"Wellington," Harry mumbled. "See if you can find it on the map, Val."

Valentina bent to the task, sorting through the growing collection of accordion-folded charts. The paper rattled in the wind from her open window. She found Interstate 70 and followed it west out of Kansas City. Lawrence, Topeka, Manhattan, Salina, Hays ... no Wellington. She backtracked and found the red line of Interstate 35. Topeka, Emporia, El Dorado, Wichita. The names had a horrifyingly familiar ring.

Valentina's finger moved further south. "Bingo. Wellington. I've go bad news for you. We're lost."

"We can't be," Harry insisted.

"We ar-re," Valentina said in a singsong voice. "Before long, we won't even be in Kansas anymore, Toto."

"Hell."

"Oklahoma, actually. The next exit is for Route 166. That's the end of the Kansas Turnpike at the Kansas-Oklahoma border."

Harry ground his teeth in irritation. "We'll take it. Plot me a route west, will you, honey?"

It cost seven dollars to escape the turnpike. As he handed over the ticket showing they'd been on the road since Kansas City, Harry quizzed the toll booth attendant. "Whatever happened to Interstate 70?"

The uniformed state employee grinned. "Seventy? You missed

that about 120 miles back." He handed Harry back change from his ten. "You can go down to the end of the cones and make a U-turn and get back on the turnpike," the man offered.

And pay another fee? "Thanks just the same, Harry said and sailed on past the cones.

"Try Route 81," Valentina suggested, refolded the map and bent to rummage in her purse.

A crossroads came up. One sign indicated Wellington. Harry bared his teeth at it. He had no wish to see that town. Instead he followed the second sign straight ahead. At least he was headed west again.

"I've been wondering if I should get hold of my Dad," Harry said. "Not Pete in Elko, but Dawud in Cairo."

Valentina popped the last of her Tic Tacs in her mouth and leaned back, her arm draped on the sill of the open window. Her blouse rippled in the wind as Harry picked up speed once more. The edge of it blew up, giving him a brief glimpse of her flat stomach and smooth skin. It was very like alabaster in tone, Harry thought, even if she didn't care for his geolological comparisons.

"To see if Dawud knows more of what Badr might be up to?" Valentina asked.

"Yeah. All I have to go on is my own impressions of how Badr and Sikina were acting the few times I saw them over this past year. As you can imagine, I kept a very low profile and didn't step outside of my narrow sphere. From work, in the museum lab to the house and back."

"With Ahmed shadowing your every move, I'll bet."

"Right on, honey."

"No one says 'right on' anymore, Harry," she admonished.

He slowed as they entered the small town of Caldwell, following the signs that led to Route 81. Signs that led south. Harry frowned but followed. Perhaps the road swung west again once they'd passed the quiet settlement. The new sign welcoming them to Oklahoma wasn't encouraging.

The road ran in conjunction with the railway, which ran alongside the huge silos of grain cooperatives. Harry glared at the tall cylinders and willed the road to turn west.

"Oh, look!" Valentina cried, and turned in her seat to stare back as they whipped past a roadside stop. "It said we're on the Chisholm Trail!"

"Yeah." Harry's voice was close to a snarl. "We're in Oklahoma, Val."

"Can't be. The map showed 81 heading north," she insisted. "It went back to Wellington and Wichita, but then we could take a road west."

The next sign, however, announced they were in Medford, Oklahoma. Harry groaned.

"I'll find another route," Valentina offered. The highway map rustled. "We're coming up on Route 64. Take that to the right," she added, and settled back to enjoy the countryside.

The vast open spaces made her a bit homesick. It had been so long since she'd been back to Nevada. Of course the tilled land of Oklahoma had nothing in common with the dry desert stretches of Nevada. And there were no mountains here, as there were back home. The land here was so flat, it looked as if a level had planed it off. There were stretches like that on the drive between Las Vegas and Reno, only, there you could catch sight of wild horses far off in the distance, rushing before the wind.

Oklahoma was settled by comparison. Very settled. The fields were tilled, showing brown and gold. It wasn't grain that Valentina thought of in connection with the state though, it was oil— Oklahoma crude. The larger fields were far to the south. But smaller oil pumps were scattered along their route, some churning away, others stilled. There were old farms, spreads with a combination of old and new buildings; there were feed lots and large pens with milling cattle.

It was beautiful and soothing to be away from the traffic. Only a few other cars and trucks passed them heading east. Harry had followed her directions correctly this time, and they were headed west. Valentina tilted her sun visor to cut the glare as the sun began to dip lower in the sky. The landscape wasn't entirely flat. The road rose and fell with dips toward streams then climbed away once more. Some spots had almost a rollercoaster feel.

There was an added attraction to this back country route. Historical markers were frequent sights. Some, it seemed, barely a mile apart. Valentina looked at them longingly, curious about the events and places they celebrated. One look at Harry's firmly set face had been enough to make her keep quiet about them. They didn't have the time to stop. She knew that. They were a long way from nowhere and the sun would soon be setting.

Small towns came and went along the way—Nash, Cherokee, Alva.

"We're still in Oklahoma," Harry said as the third village fell away behind them. "Click the heels of those ruby-red slippers and see if you can't get us back to Kansas, honey."

Valentina knocked the heels of her espadrilles together. "Buffalo," she said, her head bent over the map once more. "When you hit Buffalo, turn right on Route 183."

Harry grunted in acknowledgement and glanced at his watch. "Damn. We aren't going to get anywhere near Denver, Val. If we drive through the night, maybe ..."

"We've done that for two nights already," she pointed out. "Face it, Harry. We need to stop. You've done all the driving and need some sleep for a change."

He glanced over at her. The strain was beginning to show in his eyes. The dark circles under them weren't just smudged and sexy now, they were haggard. "Getting bossy again, are you?" His voice, at least, was amused rather than tired.

"Damn right. You promised me a bed tonight, Smith, and I'm not letting you renege on it. "

Harry stared ahead once more. "Yeah, well, I haven't seen much in the way of a motel since we got lost." His stomach growled. "Or a restaurant. Any ideas?"

Valentina smiled complacently. "Uh huh. It's about ..." She followed the twisting route on the map with her finger, counting. "... about four towns past Buffalo."

"In Kansas?"

"Absolutely."

"Relieve my mind," Harry urged. She had gotten them lost in Oklahoma, after all, he thought.

"Oh ye of little faith," Valentina muttered. Didn't he remember that he'd missed the turn for Interstate 70 and gotten them lost? "Does Dodge City meet your requirements?"

Harry slowed behind a creeping pickup truck loaded with bales of hay, waited for the road to straighten out once more, and sped up. "God, I hope so," he said.

Chapter Ten

THE SUN HAD bedded down long before their rented Corolla cruised into Dodge City. There was still a good bit of traffic. Possibly because Dodge lured tourists in search of streets once walked by the famous gunslinger/marshall, Wyatt Earp. Harry took the turn on Wyatt Earp Boulevard, turning west once more. Fortunately, when they stopped at a motel, they found there were still rooms available.

The clerk behind the counter was used to the sight of bedraggled visitors. She greeted Valentina and Harry brightly. Yes, there were vacancies. A double?

Harry picked up the pen and bent to the form the clerk pushed toward him. "Two sing ..." he began.

Valentina cut him off quickly. "Oh, no, sweetheart," she cooed contritely. "My back is really *much* better today. We don't need separate beds tonight."

The clerk smiled at Valentina and thus missed the dumbfounded look on Harry's face. "I have a room with two queen-sized beds. Perhaps that would do? Just in case your back acts up," the clerk suggested.

Valentina rewarded the woman with a big grin. "That would be perfect," she agreed.

Harry finished filling out the paperwork. The clerk looked a bit skeptical when she read his last name, but when he passed her a credit card that read *Smith* as well, the look disappeared.

Valentina took the room key and dropped it in her purse. "Is there a restaurant nearby that's still open?" she asked.

The clerk gave directions. It was only when they were seated across from each other in a booth, with plates of food before them, that Harry brought up the subject that preyed on his mind.

"If you were trying to save money in insisting on one room, Val, it wasn't necessary," he said. He cut into a pork chop. This time, however, he didn't savor the flavor. He didn't even taste it.

Valentina chased a salad tomato around before spearing it success- fully. "Oh, that wasn't why I suggested it." She grinned across the table at him then bit into the juicy red fruit.

Harry shoved another piece of pork in his mouth. "I always had a sneaking suspicion you were into sadism. You really like torturing me, don't you, Val."

"Harry," she soothed. "Why would you think that?"

"One room, coupled with the diamond engagement ring you wear," he growled.

She raised her left hand, turning it back and forth to display her now ringless fingers. "What engagement ring?"

Harry wasn't to be put off. "The one you pawned this morning. The one Todd McAllister gave you."

Valentina cut into her own chop. "Todd who?" she asked playfully.

Perturbed, Harry picked up a dinner roll, and proceeded to crumble it over his plate. "Don't do this to me, Val," he pleaded. "I'm tired and not sure what the sight of you in a nightgown would do to me."

"I didn't buy a nightgown," she said, her expression, the theatrical epitome of untouched innocence.

His jaw was clenched. "Val ..."

"Harry," she purred. Her eyes never left his face. She picked up a thick french fry and slowly licked at the catsup that dripped down it. Then she bit the end off.

His gaze trapped by the sight of Valentina's suddenly suggestive eating habits, Harry shredded the last of the bread. "I thought you wanted me to get a good night's sleep."

Valentina smiled slowly at him. Her eyes burned with green flames, like the centers of richly faceted dark emeralds. "Oh, you will," she promised huskily. "A very good night's sleep."

It was late when the call came through, but Ruskin was waiting. Dodge City. Why had Smith deviated from his course, Ruskin wondered? After sticking to the Interstate, he'd verged off of it to head south.

The sergeant pulled out a map and checked the routes out of Dodge. The way would be circuitous, but Smith might be making for Amarillo, Texas. Or Albuquerque in New Mexico. Or Pueblo, Colorado.

He picked up the phone and dialed quickly. "It's Ruskin," he said. "Just got the lastest call. Dodge City, Kansas. He's deviated from the original course a bit, but hasn't come to roost yet." He waited, listening to the smooth answer, disappointed when it didn't include an invitation. "Yes, of course I will," he agreed at last and rang off.

Ruskin stared at the phone a moment longer, then punched a second number. A sleepy, gruff voice barked at him. "This is Ruskin. Smith just called in, Lieutenant. He's in Kansas. And he wants a favor."

Sikina replaced the receiver gently and smiled to herself. Hadi might have confused Cole Ruskin, but her cousin hadn't deceived her. She had tracked his flight quite easily since making friends with the police sergeant. The computer hacker she'd picked up at a local computer dealership was of even more help. Through his terminal she had discovered Hadi's change of automobiles in Ohio. The records showed the Toyota Corolla hadn't been turned in yet. Her new friend had checked Boston, in the event that Hadi had actually gone where he'd told the agency he was bound, then St. Louis and Kansas City. She was sure that Hadi would change vehicles again before reaching his destination.

She had no doubt as to what that destination would be. So sure, in fact, that she had called ahead, sending Iz'al on to complete arrangements. Sattam would be watching at the airport in Denver. If her cousin changed cars again there, Sattam would follow Hadi. Unless, that is, the fool allowed her surprisingly evasive cousin to escape him once again.

Sikina smoothed the frown from her brow and placed one last call.

Badr stood at the edge of the site staring out over the ruins. The

Temple of 'Awwam was ghostly, bathed in the light of the deity it honored. The ancients had built their sacred places to ask for favors and blessings. Burnt offerings and blood sacrifices had stained the sanctuaries. Gifted oracles had delivered messages, translating the wishes of the deity to the worshippers.

In the moonlight it was almost possible to see the wraiths of the ancient ones prostrating themselves, bowing and scraping to each of the four directions of the compass.

Of course, they hadn't had a compass. Hadn't had the knowledge of the one God, Allah. Now devout men faced only one direction; they faced toward the holy city of Mecca in Saudi Arabia.

He had prayed to Allah, the Beneficent, the Merciful, for knowlege of Bilqis. Even if she had been just a woman, the proof of her existence was important. The Prophet had written briefly of her, refusing to use her name. The tale was recounted in the twenty-seventh chapter, in the story of the Ant. A report had be relayed to Sulaiman, son of Dawood, as he sat on his throne in the northern provinces. "... I found a woman ruling over them, and she has been given abundance and she has a mighty throne." The queen and her people worshipped the light-giving orbs in the sky, the sun and the moon, instead of Allah, and "... Shaitan has made their deeds fair-seeming to them ..." Sulaiman had been aghast and determined to save them, even if it took trickery and magic to do so. The heathen queen was due to visit his court. There was little time. "O chiefs!" the great Sulaiman had cried, "which of you can bring to me her throne before they come to me in submission?" A *jinn* had answered the call, whisking the queen's throne to Sulaiman's court "in the twinkling of an eye." When Bilqis arrived she was deceived, not realizing they had tampered with her throne, seeing the palace floor as one would a shallow lake through which she must wade. Finding her woman's intellect bested by the superior one of Sulaiman and the power of his God, she called to the king. "My Lord! surely I have been unjust to myself, and I submit with Sulaiman to Allah, the Lord of the worlds."

Badr knew especially these words of the Koran by heart. But he doubted Bilqis had actually prostrated herself before Allah; the seasons of the moon had too great a pull for her. Long after

116

Sulaiman's court had disappeared in the desert sands, the open, oval temple to 'Awwam continued to draw the devout.

Badr stood there now, wondering if perhaps the old god was more than just a remnant of an ancient world. Perhaps where Bilqis was concerned, 'Awwam's protection was more powerful than Allah's intervention. It was the thought of a heretic. But in the moonlight, at the ruins of the lunar deity's temple, it was a tempting premise. He could almost smell the incense, fresh from the caravan trail, burning on the altar.

The columns, some fallen, some leaning, some still standing, were like sentries. Badr had thought them so when he stood beneath their early morning shadow and listened to his father direct the excavation. The fine ashlar masonry wall had seemed taller then. As large and stalwart as Yussuf al-Hashid's reputation. The wall appeared to have shrunk now, but his father's accomplishments still loomed over him.

But not for long, Badr promised himself. Soon, his moment in the limelight would come, and it would make his father's finds insignificant by comparison.

Eliot Faraday hung back. The numbing despair he'd felt on the mountain was fading, helped in a large part by catching sight of Badr al-Hashid on the street in Sirwah. He should be surprised that the man was this near Marib, but he wasn't. Hashid seemed the kind of man who went his own way. The fools at the hospital had probably discontinued the medication that kept Badr helpless. Once drugs no longer chained him to the bed, Hashid had merely checked himself out—without the offices of any of the hospital staff, most likely. Faraday kept to the shadows, watching the still figure as Badr stared out over the archaeological site. Sikina's husband was dressed in the disreputable garb of a workman but his carriage belied the disguise. No one would take him for one of the *fellahin*. His step was too arrogant, his shoulders too squared to have suffered deprivation.

What did Badr al-Hashid see when he looked out over the moon-bathed ruins? His attitude was nearly reverent. The Judeo-Christian world stuck by its Ten Commandments, one of which, if Faraday remembered his Sunday school lessons of long ago, was an admonition against the worship of false gods. The Five Pillars of Islam didn't spell it out that clearly. Perhaps the Prophet Mohammad had men like Badr al-Hashid in mind when he wrote them down.

The first was merely a delaration that "there is no God but God and Mohammad is his prophet." A good shyster could argue that around to Badr's favor. All he had to do was claim the ancient deities were akin to the *jinns*, those fairy tale creatures that appeared as regularly in the Koran as angels did in the Bible.

The second Pillar was prayer. Faraday had watched the men of the Islamic world bring business to an abrupt halt five times a day. At dawn, noon, mid-afternoon, sunset, and night, the high carrying call of the *muezzin* came from the tops of the minarets of the mosques. Dark-robed women stood in the shadows, making their own silent obeisance. But the men were on their knees, prostrate as they observed daily prayers.

The third duty involved the fast. Supposedly it reminded the faithful of their less fortunate brothers. Faraday hadn't seen that it made any big difference. Nor had the fourth, the *zakat* or alms-giving. There were still too many poor in the oil-rich Middle East. Not that he cared what happened to the beggars. Faraday practiced a religion of self. What he didn't have, he was determined to get. Any any price.

Badr's visit to the temple ruins had the aura of a pilgrimage. Not as blessed as the *Hajj*, the final duty of all Mohammadans to visit Mecca, preferably in the month of *Dhu-l-Hijja*, but certainly carrying the same thoughtful air of homage. In the silver glow of the moon, surrounded by the tall shadows of an ancient world, Badr looked like a man balanced between two religions. Faraday wondered which he would choose, that of Allah or that of greed.

When Badr left the site, Faraday followed quietly through the streets of Sirwah until Hashid slid within the door of a tall, old stone house. The American doctor settled himself in an adjacent doorway to watch. He was close. He could feel it, almost taste it on the cool night breeze as it came off the mountain.

Faraday knew Badr al-Hashid had made his decision. The visit to the ruins had merely been a reaffirmation. Badr had sold his soul to Shaitan in return for the wealth of an ancient queen.

She was as beautiful as a *houri* strayed out of paradise.

As a child curled at the feet of the women in Sirwah, Harry had listened to tales of beings like Valentina. She was lovely enough to tempt any *jinn* to whisk her away to his harem. Then Harry himself would have to descend to the fifth level of the earth, into the world of the supernatural, the land of the *Djinn*, where no human dared tread. (Except perhaps an intrepid, love-sick, spelunking geologist.) Like all the brave heroes he'd heard about late at night, all the sumptuous delights in the world of the immortals would not lure him from his quest. Birds with golden plumage didn't interest him. He could ignore the banquets, always laid for forty since the days of Noah. He would trick any *jinn*, con any *efreet*, deceive any ghoul who held her prisoner within their palaces of silver and gold bricks. He would overcome all misfortunes to rescue her, and carry her away to safety in the world above, the mortal world of the *Ins*. Valentina was meant to recline within the billowing folds of his tent, against cushions of the finest silk, to tread on carpets that rivalled mountain wild flowers in color and design. As a desert prince, a scion of the mighty Bakils, he would ply her with the plumpest of dates, offer her the sweetest of spring water.

Perhaps fairy tales did come true. If he cast Todd McAllister as the evil *jinn*—which Loretta Crosby was obviously willing to do—then he had carried off the prized maiden. In lieu of a picturesque Bedouin tent, he'd provided an American motel room complete with television and air conditioning. She wasn't dressed in diaphanous harem pants and transparent veils. Instead, Valentina wore a slightly damp, very thin, hotel towel. She reclined against pillows that lost their shape quickly, amid rumpled percale sheets. Rather than dates she popped fluffy pieces of cheese-flavored popcorn into her mouth.

When Valentina smiled up at him, her lips curved slowly, sensuously. Her eyes were the slightest bit heavy-lidded, giving her the appearance of a very contented, satisfied *houri*.

He had done his best, starting with a shared shower and a thorough testing of the bed springs. And soon, he'd prove his worthiness once again. Very soon.

Harry kicked the door closed behind him and carried the plastic container of ice over to the dresser. He dropped a cube or two in each of the glasses provided by the management and poured the Seven Up he'd bought at the vending machine at the end of the corridor.

He heard the sigh of the bed springs and smelled the aroma of popcorn behind him.

"Mmm. Bubbly," Valentina purred at his shoulder.

"The real stuff when we hit Vegas," Harry promised. He turned and handed her a cup.

She was still in a playful mood and entwined her arm with his to sip it. She had to stand on tip toe so as not to spill it. Some dribbled down her chin anyway. Harry bent to lick it away and ended by kissing her again.

Quite a while later they were curled upon the bed watching the final guest of the evening chat with Johnny Carson. The bag of popcorn lay on Harry's chest. Valentina's towel was flung where Harry had tossed it on the pristine cover of the second bed. Valentina had pulled the sheet up to cover her breast but it slipped often as she wiggled around reaching for her glass of soda or into the bag of popcorn. Harry's own clothing lay in a forgotten heap on the floor.

"You don't think they forgot us, do you?" Valentina asked, her head comfortably cushioned on Harry's shoulder.

"Who?"

"The police. Who did you think I meant?"

"Oh, them." He was too relaxed, too euphoric to worry. "Sergeant Ruskin took the call. Since it's mid-morning already in Cairo he should be able to catch Dad at the museum. He'll call when he's got the information."

Valentina stared at the television screen. An airline commercial went by, then a public service notice from the Army that urged her to be all that she could be. Perhaps it was time to start deciding how she could be all that she wanted to be. What did that involve? Long ago it had meant becoming an archaeologist. More recently it had merely been getting through each day, processing a certain number of letters during daylight, following Todd's wishes in the evening. Or rather his instructions. Todd never really expressed anything as a request. He issued moderately phrased orders.

Now Todd was not going to figure in her future. The real question was, did she want Harry to be part of it?

"Harry? Remember how it was when we were at school?"

He gathered her close, turning to kiss the delectable tip of her nose. The bag of popcorn spilled on the bed between them. They both ignored it. "Wonderful memories," he murmured. "We'd study in bed and take frequent breaks." He kissed her eyelids.

"We were happy, weren't we? For a while?"

"Val ..."

"Why did things start going downhill for us, Harry? Was it me?"

When he didn't answer immediately, Valentina pressed harder. "I wasn't pretty enough."

"Never."

"I was too anti-social."

"You were working hard on your degree, honey."

Valentina wasn't finished though. "I didn't pay enough attention to you, did I?"

Harry sighed deeply. He couldn't just brush that statement away. He *had* felt left out. Too many times. She'd seemed more interested in a dead civilization than she had been in him.

Valentina was snuggled against his chest. Only the thin sheet and the crumbs of crushed popcorn were between them. Her lashes sheltered her eyes so that he couldn't read the hurt in them.

"Nonsense, Val," Harry insisted, perhaps a shade too heartily. "We were the perfect couple. Everybody said so." It was true, he thought. He'd never seen so many stunned expressions as when she left him. Their friends only accepted the breakup when the days turned into weeks and then into months. None of them were surprised that he hadn't found another woman. When he saw them, which he still did at least once a year, Denny and Gene kidded, calling him lucky, a confirmed bachelor. They had both married the co-eds they'd been dating back then. But Harry hadn't felt lucky. He'd felt doomed.

Her lashes fluttered. She looked up, meeting his eyes. "If we were so perfect, how come you never said the words I wanted to hear?" she asked quietly.

He hadn't thought them necessary back then. He'd thought she knew he loved her. "We were so close, so in tune," he said. Beneath the sheet, his hand lingered on her bare skin, traced the too prominent edges of her ribs, the sharp line of her hip bone. "I thought you could see into my heart, could read my mind. What words did you want to hear, Val?"

Her eyes flickered, moving gently over his face as if comparing her memories to the reality; as if she were memorizing his features against the future. Her gaze lingered on his mouth. She ran a finger tip tenderly along his bottom lip.

"Marry me," she whispered.

Harry bent his mouth to hers. "I'd love to," he murmured against her lips.

When they parted Valentina was breathless. "I was merely telling you what I once wanted you to say," she claimed. But her eyes glimmered more brightly than he'd ever seen them before.

He armed himself against hurt, taking refuge in teasing. "Putting words in my mouth, huh?"

"No, I ..."

"Trying to renege already, Val?"

She stared into the beautiful blue of his eyes once more, seeking to see beyond the light-hearted tone of his words. Despite the soft amused curve of his lips, Harry was tensing. His heart pounded fast and hard against her breast. Valentina made a decision. She slid her arms around his neck. "Would you please marry me, Harry?" she asked sweetly. "I don't think I want to face another future without you."

His hand moved lower under the covers, molding her against him. "I can't give you diamonds like McAllister did," he warned.

"They're just rocks."

"My contract is up. I'm unemployed."

Amusement crinkled the corners of Valentina's eyes. "Me, too. I'm not going back to Washington. Do you think we can live just on love?"

"That or food stamps," he said huskily and kissed her, his caress as urgent and hungry as it had been earlier.

The ringing of the phone delayed any further celebration. Harry rolled over, pulling Valentina with him. She lay contently on top of him, only slightly aware that the sheet no longer covered her naked form.

"Smith," Harry drawled cupping the receiver to his ear.

Valentina ran a teasing finger along his jawline. The prickle of his beard was rough but she didn't mind. She smoothed the drooping sides of his mustache.

Harry smiled gently at her. He adjusted his position so that Valentina slipped to rest intimately between his legs. She raised perfectly shaped brows in exaggerated surprise and twitched a bit closer.

In Washington, Sergeant Ruskin frowned at his phone. Smith sounded far too relaxed for a man running for his life.

"So what did my father say?" the fugitive asked. At Ruskin's answer, Harry started up abruptly, causing Valentina's chin to hit his chest sharply. "What did you say?" he demanded, his voice no longer lazy or content.

Ruskin's voice was loud enough for Valentina to hear it this time. "I said your father wasn't there," he repeated. "He got a call two days ago and left the museum. According to one of the guards, he looked distracted. No one has seen him since. There is no answer at his home. It appears," Ruskin claimed, his voice winding down now in frustration, "that Dawud al-Bakil has also disappeared."

Chapter Eleven

THE DRIVE TO Denver was peaceful. Or would have been if Harry and Valentina hadn't been worried about their relatives. Badr al-Hashid had escaped all efforts of the San'a' police to locate him. Dawud al-Bakil had disappeared quickly, as if he'd been plucked from the streets of Cairo by a *ghouleh* to serve as main course on her dinner table. When Valentina had asked Ruskin for word of her grandmother, the pattern seemed set. Loretta Crosby had not telephoned to tell them where she was. Despite a series of calls to Loretta's closest cronies, Valentina had been unable to find a trace of her grandmother.

Harry hadn't been very successful in comforting her. His mind was on the disappearance of his father.

They sped out of Dodge City along Route 50. Just as it had when they'd stumbled into Oklahoma, the railroad ran in tandem with the road again. The tall silos of the cooperatives had decorated the skyline in Dodge. Now they shadowed the smaller settlements of Cimarron, Ingalls and Pierceville. The feed lots grew larger. Pen upon pen of milling cattle awaited transport to butchering facilities around the country.

The landscape seemed endless. Fields stretched out from horizon to horizon. How long had it been since civilization had risen on all sides of them with steel and concrete structures that touched the sky? Kansas City? It seemed much longer than twenty-four hours since they'd been there. So much had happened. Yesterday, Valentina mused, she'd worn a diamond ring and been engaged to an ambitious politician. Today the ring was gone and *she'd* asked an unemployed geologist to spend his life with her. Her heart sang at the prospect.

"Let's be logical about all this, Val," Harry urged as they followed the gentle winding curves through more farm land. "The map is the key. Right?"

"Absolutely." Valentina took a bite of the bright red apple she'd bought at the convenience store while Harry was filling the Corolla's gas tank. A few more goodies rested in a bag at her feet.

"But the only people who could conceivably know of its existence are Badr, Sikina, and myself."

"And whoever tried to kill you," Valentina pointed out. "Although Sikina might have been in Washington the day of the museum reception, she wasn't at the party. You would have seen her. But someone was who knew about the treasure because they shot at us. They wouldn't have known we were on the patio unless they were among the guests."

Harry nodded. "So who could be working with Sikina? The two men who showed up at your house weren't exactly the type to take orders from a woman."

"I didn't really see them. Things sorta took off when I arrived," Valentina said.

"Sorta took off?" Harry grimaced. One of the assassins had been killed, Ahmed had been wounded, and Valentina herself had missed death by inches. The memory of the *jambiya* sunk to the hilt in the wall still haunted him.

"I was being modest, Harry," she insisted. She sounded proud rather than modest. "So, if the men weren't taking orders from Sikina, it means that they are working for a man."

"A man who's Sikina's partner." Harry pondered a moment. He slowed for the next little town, creeping through at a sedate twenty-five miles an hour. "If Sikina is in the States and the treasure is still in Yemen, does that mean her partner is still there?"

"Good question. If he is, could he have kidnapped your dad and Badr?"

Harry frowned at the rear bumper of the car in front of him. It had a very faded bumper sticker urging him to vote for Ronald Reagan. "I don't think so, Val. If this hypothetical guy had Badr, he doesn't need the map."

Valentina bit into her apple. Her tongue flicked out to catch a stray drop of juice at the corner of her mouth. "Sounds logical to me. But since your dad has now disappeared, it doesn't sound as if he does have Badr, does it?"

"Why Dad, though?"

"Because they think he knows about the map."

"Which he doesn't. I didn't even share it with Pete Smith, and I was one hell of a lot closer to him than to Dawud when I was a kid."

"But do they know that?"

"Hell. Why isn't this getting any easier? We should have been able to narrow things down by now." He was silent, turning his attention to traffic as they followed the route through Garden City. Once more out among the fields, Harry sped up.

Valentina finished her apple and moved on to a bag of pretzels. She didn't look like a girl who'd wolfed down a Belgian waffle and a dish of strawberries earlier. "Do you think they've got Grandma?" She rushed on before he could answer, afraid of what he might say. "I don't really think they could. I mean, Grandma said she planned to disappear and she has done just that. She's probably enjoying herself immensely. I just wish I knew where she was."

"Maybe she'll call Konig and Ruskin today, honey," Harry soothed.

She tapped a pretzel against her teeth thoughtfully. "You know, it doesn't make any sense really for them to take hostages. They have no way to get in touch with us. They don't know where to call. It isn't like they'd call the police in Washington and leave a message."

"True. If Loretta is lying low with friends, and Badr has wandered off into hiding because someone tried to kill him, that leaves us with only one puzzling disappearance. What happened to Dad?"

Valentina sucked the salt off her pretzel. "Er ... he isn't in the habit of picking up strange women?"

"He never found one stranger than my mother," Harry said, his voice amused. "No, I don't think he's shacked up, Val."

"Well, it was worth a shot. He can't be off on museum business.

They'd know about it."

"Leave it. We don't have enough facts to sort it out yet. Perhaps when we check in with Washington they'll have more information for us."

Valentina hated to give up just yet, but couldn't see any way to gnaw on this bone successfully at the moment. "So we wait now, huh?"

"Yep. 'Fraid so."

"I wonder who the man back in Arabia is?" Valentina pondered. "Another Yemeni?"

Harry shrugged. "Could be, but I doubt it."

"Why?"

"Logic," he said. "Have you got another apple in that bag?"

Valentina handed over the fruit. "Explain the logic, please. Why don't you think Sikina's sweetheart is Arabian?"

Harry sank his teeth into the apple. It spritzed his mustache with juice. "Simple. Sikina's in Washington. No Arab man would have let her leave the country. He would have wheedled the information out of her, then dumped her. Therefore, the man has to be European or American. He hired local assassins, but he put Sikina in charge of operations here. Because the hired help isn't used to kowtowing to a woman, they have flubbed up each attempt to get my share of the map." Harry grinned ahead at the road and took another bite of his apple. "He's probably seething right now."

Eliot Faraday wasn't seething. He was stiff and uncomfortable. Badr al-Hashid hadn't left the house. What was he waiting for, Faraday wondered? Had he hired workmen to unearth the treasure? If so, how could Faraday himself get the find away from them?

He'd hunched in the doorway all night, staring sleeplessly at the old, stone house. Three stories tall, it had stood for generations. A number of other homes abutted it, making the lane itself appear narrow. All the streets in this section of the city seemed to wind in snake-like configurations. Faraday had nearly lost sight of Badr the night before as the archaeologist worked his way through alleyways, slinking from one shadow to the next.

When the sun had risen, and the woman of the household within whose doorway he sheltered had come forth with her shopping basket, Faraday had sauntered on, trying to look like a tourist. He'd pretended to study the tall, square stone houses and the lush growth peeping above the garden walls. He'd heard children at play, women chattering. As if lost, Faraday had wandered on until he felt he was indeed lost.

It was only as he wended his way back to Hashid's refuge that he began to recognize features in the town.

Faraday stepped into the shelter of yet another doorway and pulled the map fragment from his shirt pocket. The narrow path he'd been following nearly matched one of the twisting lines on the page. The mark lead toward the torn edge. It seemed slightly darker than the others sketched, as if it had been drawn over carefully to denote importance.

Faraday followed the winding route past where it ended abruptly on the map and found himself back outside the tall, closed house where Badr al-Hashid had gone to ground. The red-haired man smiled triumphantly. He was more than just close now. Staring at the closed door and shuttered windows of the old house, he could almost see the balance in his Swiss bank account rise.

Ruskin had dressed in his best suit, a three-piece job in a deep navy that fit all occasions. His tie was a subtle combination of dark blue and maroon. He hoped it looked Ivy League. His shirt was a softer shade of carmine. He'd spent a couple bucks to have his black tasselled loafers buffed to a mirror finish.

He had to knock twice before the door opened at Sikina's hotel suite. When it did he stared blankly at the uniformed maid who looked an inquiry at him.

"Sergeant Ruskin, Washington P.D.," he told her and flashed his badge. "Is Mrs. Hashid in?"

The woman didn't move back or invite him in. She stood blocking his way. "The lady who stayed here?" she asked.

"Yes. Mrs. Sikina Hashid."

"Foreign lady," the maid mused and shook her head. "Checked out. Otherwise I wouldn't be here, would I?"

"Checked out?" Ruskin repeated a bit dazed. "When?"

"Last night." She tried to shut the door, but Ruskin stopped it with an insistent hand.

"When last night?" he snapped.

"I wouldn't know. Check with the desk, why don't you? I've got work to do, you know," the maid whined. This time he let her close the door.

The front desk wasn't much help even when he produced his badge. Sikina had left. She had paid her bill. They only hoped that Mrs. Hashid would choose to honor them with her lovely presence again.

Ruskin returned to his desk at the police station. He wasn't scheduled to be on duty yet. In order to cover the phones for incoming calls from both their fugitives and the authorities in Yemen, he and Konig had split the shifts. Since Konig had a family and rank, he'd taken the day shifts leaving Ruskin the nights. With an eight hour time difference between Washington and San'a', that left the bulk of the calls to Ruskin. He hadn't minded. It broke up the time when he wasn't called out on a new homicide.

Although the business day had ended in the Middle East, Ruskin got back on the phone. The accounting department would be down on him for overseas charges when the bills came in, but that didn't matter. What mattered was saving his neck.

It took only a moment for the Washington airport to confirm that Sikina Hashid had indeed left the city. Ruskin was surprised at her destination. Sikina had taken the first flight out, bound for Las Vegas, Nevada. He puzzled over her destination a moment, then, with a glimmer of an idea, he pulled out the dossiers Konig had compiled on Harry Smith and the Crosby women. Income tax records showed that Smith and Valentina Crosby had attended school at the university in Las Vegas.

A few more calls, both to the airlines and the police departments in San'a' and Cairo filled in the rest of the information.

Ruskin stared at his scrawled batch of notes a moment, then picked up the scattered, loose sheets and printouts and stormed down the aisle toward Konig's office.

Harry and Valentina shot off Route 287 in Limon, Colorado, and headed toward Denver on Interstate 70 once more. When the exchange for 225 came up in Aurora, Harry took it, heading for the airport. Although they had not noticed anyone following them, both Harry and Valentina had decided they wouldn't take a chance. They'd had the Toyota Corolla for over a thousand miles (neither cared to count up how many more had been added with their unexpected detour into Oklahoma). It was past time to muddy the trail.

At Stapleton International Airport, Harry cruised into the rental car lot and handed over the keys. He and Valentina took the shuttle to the main terminal and found a restaurant. They both ordered Bloody Marys and began to relax a bit.

Lunch consisted of neatly cut, generously stacked club sandwiches. This time Valentina didn't play with her french fries. She was too busy talking.

"What do you mean you don't know much about Bilqis? If she was the Queen of Saba, aren't there history books written about her?"

Harry chewed slowly on the stalk of celery from his drink. The crunch was loud and crisp. He bit off another section. "No, there aren't. That's what has always been so fascinating about her to Badr. There's not much more than a legend or so."

"Where there's a legend there has to be some truth," Valentina argued. "It's been three thousand years since she's supposed to have lived. That's a long time for a story to get passed down, Harry."

"It's also a damn long time in which to lose any trace of fact about a person or event, Val."

She pulled the cellophane tasselled toothpick out of one wedge of her sandwich and pointed it at him. "I'm not talking about the story, the legend itself. Just the fact that her name has survived has got to mean something."

"No, it doesn't," Harry insisted around a mouthful of food. "Look at Arthur Pendragon. That's only a couple hundred years."

Valentina wasn't about to give in. "There may not have been a King Arthur or a Camelot as depicted in the tales of the Round Table, but there is historical evidence that a chieftain, possibly named Arturus, led Anglo-Romans against invading Norsemen. Maybe somewhere around 1500 years ago, give or take a hundred here or there. That's half the time that has elapsed since Badr's girlfriend reigned."

She paused to sip her Bloody Mary. She wrinkled her nose. Too much Tabasco for her taste, but that didn't stop her from taking a second swallow.

"Is there nothing other than these legends to say that Bilqis existed?" she pressed.

Harry chewed thoughtfully. "Other than the Bible and the Koran, you mean?"

Valentina choked on a bit of pickle. "She's in scripture?"

"Oh, not by name, honey. Her name is part of legend."

"But, Harry, if she's mentioned in not one but two holy books, surely that lends credence to her historical existence."

He shook his head slowly and polished off the last bite of his club sandwich. "Come on, Val. We both read the same book: *Archaeology of the Bible*. Remember? You even did a book report on it. What did it say?"

"About what in particular? There was a lot about cross references to Egyptian state records, the interesting tidbit about how the story of the flood, Noah and the Ark, was predated by the Sumarian story of a world-wide flood in the story of Gilgamesh. And the excavation levels of the tells ..."

Harry held up a hand to stop the flow. "I thought you weren't interested in archaeology anymore?"

Valentina's eyes glowed with enthusiasm. "I'm considering taking it up again."

Harry wondered if now was the time to tell her of his own plans to specialize in that same milieu, then thought better of it. Discussions about their future together would have to wait until the adventure was over.

"Think about Solomon then, Val," he urged. "What did it say about the most celebrated judge of the ancient world? The man who supposedly owned mines of untold wealth?"

Valentina frowned in thought. She fingered the leaves of the celery stalk in her drink. "Mmm. Very little evidence that he existed, huh."

"Some possibly in tell excavations but nil in any of the surviving records of the civilizations that ringed the kingdom of Jerusalem. Even three thousand years ago there was an international trade market. According to the Bible, Solomon is supposed to have had a trade fleet manned by Phoenicians. Egypt imported myrrh and frankincense from Arabian traders. Myrrh was used in the mummification process, so its availability was very important. The records show imports, but they don't mention a queen."

"And they should. Is that what you're getting at?"

"If Bilqis indeed existed, there should be some record, some kind of evidence. She is said to have ruled at Marib, the center of Saba's commerce. In the middle of the caravan route, Val. I've always thought Badr was chasing bubbles over this. As soon as he thought he had a lead, it would burst in his face, leaving him more and more bitter."

Valentina pushed her plate back. As had been her habit the last few days, she'd barely left a crumb on it. "I can see where proving her existence would be a coup for Badr," she said. "But I agree with you. There really never was a hope that he would ever find evidence. If she's not mentioned by name in the Bible or the Koran, then they could be talking about different monarchs in different time periods."

Harry pushed back his chair. "Well, not exactly, Val," he said. "You see the same guy is involved each time. The wise Sulaiman of the Koran is the same as Solomon of the Bible. And Bilqis ..." He drew a long breath, as if reluctant to add to the story. "Bilqis is known in both as the Queen of Sheba."

Chapter Twelve

VALENTINA WAITED UNTIL they were out of the restaurant to explode. "Sheba! Solomon and Sheba?"

"Uh, yeah." Harry tried to drag her down the concourse back to where the desks for rental cars were located. Valentina refused to budge.

"*The* Solomon and Sheba?" she repeated, still a bit stunned. "This puts a whole different perspective on the thing, Harry."

"Val," he muttered under his breath. "Would you move? You're blocking traffic."

She let him manhandle her arm, guiding her through the terminal. The two backpacks Harry carried bobbed against his legs. The extra shopping bag, overflowing with her purchases, knocked against Valentina's. "Just think what this would mean to the world if Badr's really found something this time!" Valentina said in awe.

"Mean? You make it sound like he's Alan Quartermaine hot on the trail of King Solomon's mines. Rider Haggard made that story up honey. There's no truth in it."

Valentina's stride matched his now. Harry dropped her arm but entwined his fingers with hers. "Is the story the same?" she asked.

"In Haggard's book and the movies?"

She gave him a look of disdain. "In the Bible and the Koran."

"Not quite. It sounds more like a fairy tale in the Koran, but that's probably only because there's a *jinn* in it. Legend says that Solomon, or rather Sulaiman, reviewed an assembly of birds but the hoopoe was playing hookey. Threatened with punishment, the hoopoe comes up with a tale of a queen in the mighty province of Saba, or rather Sheba. This feathered slacker claims that the people aren't worshipping Allah but are mighty fond of the sun."

They neared the area in which the rental desks were lined up, one eager company after another. Harry slowed his step. Until he got the story out, he knew Valentina would give him no peace.

"Actually evidence shows a preference for the moon. There's a large temple outside of Sirwah. Anyway, Bilqis, or Sheba, if you will, goes to visit Sulaiman and ends up praising the one God, Allah, the Beneficent, the Merciful. In the Bible, she just stops by because she's heard of Solomon's great wisdom and brings him gifts of goodies from her successful caravan import business. She's the ancient counterpart of a high-powered woman executive set on developing new accounts. The Biblical story is much shorter than the one in the Koran, but it isn't as gussied up either."

Valentina mused over the information. "I need a library," she said. Harry recognized the glow in her eyes, the flush on her cheeks. Valentina was hooked.

"Not yet you don't. First we need to get to Vegas."

"Ah ha! So we are going there! I knew it. I even know why!" she crowed smugly. "The annual baseball game and barbecue with Northrup and company."

"They need a shortstop."

"Like a hole in the head. I'm guessing you haven't improved your game over the years."

"You've got a vicious tongue, Val Crosby. Are you sure you were planning on sharing McAllister's political career? Lord, you'd have lost him his office before the next election," Harry grumbled.

Valentina twinkled up at him. "Guess I wasn't cut out to be a politician's wife after all. How do you think I'll do as a geologist's mate?"

The nice thing about airports, Harry thought fleetingly is that people are always saying hello and goodbye and doing it with a lot of hugging and kissing. And no one seemed to mind. He took advantage of this pleasant phenomenon and put his arms around Valentina. The double set of backpacks in his hand now brushed against the back of her thighs but Valentina barely noticed them.

"How do you think you'd handle being an archaeologist's better half?" he asked.

Her smile was a combination of surprise, wonder, and approval. "I think I could handle that very well," Valentina said softly.

"It won't be a particularly profitable profession, Val. I'm planning to specialize in the petrography angle. There won't be any limit to the places we'll go. We could end up on the Navaho reservation studying your beloved Anasazi or back in Yemen or the Yucatan or Yonkers. My field will be narrow, but the time spans I work in will be endless. From prehistoric to modern potters, I will scrutinize their works under my microscope. I might even end up teaching."

Valentina stood on tiptoe and lightly brushed her lips against his. "Stop trying to talk me out of it," she said. "You know I've always had a weakness for pottery."

Harry grinned happily, relieved that she was pleased with the change he was planning to make in his career. "Only a weakness, Val?" he teased. "I thought you even dreamed about ... Oh, shit!"

Before Valentina realized what was happening, Harry had dragged her behind a crowd of waiting passengers.

"What ...?"

"The *qayn*," he hissed.

"Is that English?"

Harry eased further back and took a calming breath. It didn't work. He dropped the overstuffed backpacks on the floor. His nerves prickled. His stomach knotted.

"The guy who got away in Washington. He's here," Harry whispered urgently.

"The one who threw that knife at me?" Valentina was breathless, but rather than radiate fear, she bloomed with suppressed excitement. "Where?"

Against his better judgement, Harry described the assassin and what he was wearing. Valentina dropped her own bag next to the backpacks and moseyed to the edge of the crowd, pretending to study the list of incoming and outgoing aircraft.

"He's got really bad taste in clothes, doesn't he?" she said when she returned to Harry's side. "Do you think he spotted you?"

Harry's eyes narrowed. "What do you mean did he spot *me*? He's seen both of us before, Val."

"Not really. He'd know you. But I don't think he'd know me from

Adam. Or rather Eve. He just threw that knife at a sound, not at a person. Then he ran."

Harry thought back over the events of Saturday afternoon. If he remembered the sequence correctly, there was a good chance the man hadn't gotten a clear look at Valentina. She'd barreled down the stairs, just a mad rush of sound as far as the man was concerned. He'd thrown without sighting, thank goodness. The assassin's eyes had turned immediately to his fallen comrade and then he'd been gone with a fleetness a *saluki*, a desert greyhound, would have envied. Harry studied the stubborn thrust of her chin, the gentle wisps of caramel-colored hair that framed her face, the direct way her alluring green eyes looked at the world. What man could ignore such beauty?

'He can't have forgotten you, honey," Harry insisted.

Valentina preened at his words. "Lots of men dismiss me from their thoughts."

"Not healthy ones."

"How sweet, Harry. But you really don't have to worry. I'll bet I could go up and rent a car at the counter in front of him and he wouldn't notice."

Harry ran a hand through his hair. "I'm not taking a chance on that, Val. Let's say I'm only half convinced he wouldn't recognize you."

"He won't." She was sure of herself. "Maybe if I was dressed the same he'd have a glimmer. But I'm not." Valentina pirouetted, her arms slightly spread. "See? No Redskins T-shirt, no jeans, no hightops."

He'd already admired the bright-red walking shorts and long-waisted sunset gold vest. A jaunty scarf, tied loosely around her neck, picked up the same vibrant colors in a design that looked like splattered paint. Valentina's freshly washed hair bounced with life, swinging with each step she took. Many men had followed her progress through the airport, but he had to agree, the vigilant assassin probably wouldn't connect her with the harridan who'd waved an empty gun at him three days ago.

"Okay," Harry sighed. "But instead of a car, get airline tickets. The next flight out to Vegas."

Valentina stood on tiptoe to kiss him lightly. "I knew you'd see it my way," she declared and pranced off, quite pleased with herself.

Left behind with the backpacks and shopping bag, Harry ground his teeth in frustration. The man he'd insulted Saturday, terming

136

him a *qayn*, a man of low status and non-Arab descent, still lounged far too close for Harry's comfort. The man hadn't even followed Valentina with his eyes when she walked past. For the guy to ignore a woman like Val proved he'd been right in this estimation of the thug, Harry decided. The man was a *qayn*. That or a eunuch.

Valentina was back with the tickets within a few minutes. The next flight was an hour away yet. Harry gnawed on his lower lip nervously. He could see the assassin from where he stood, but the crowd was thinning and soon the man was bound to notice him.

"Let's phone Washington again. Even if they haven't got news for us, we've got some for them," Harry said.

Valentina picked up her shopping bag, leaving the heavier backpacks for him to carry. "Okay. I'll be your lookout," she offered brightly.

Her cheerfulness was beginning to irritate him.

Konig was in his office when the call went through. Harry breathed a sigh of relief. "This is Smith. Val and I are in Denver. Did you get a clean set of fingerprints off that knife?"

The police lieutenant didn't balk at the swift change of subject. "The one in the wall? Yeah. No match yet although we've checked Interpol's files as well. Why?"

" 'Cause the man you want is here!" Harry said, his voice low but vibrant with suppressed tension. "Lord, we almost walked into him!"

"Where?" Konig snapped.

"Airport."

"I'll call the Denver police and have them put out an APB based on your description of him."

Harry looked back in the direction of the rental desks. Valentina was standing farther down the concourse so that she could keep her eye on the man. "Shit. It'll take them too long to get here," he groaned into the receiver. "Listen, I'll think of something to delay him. But Val and I are out of here within the hour. We're not sticking around to identify the guy."

Konig was quiet a moment. "All right," he said at last. "But this time, tell me where you're headed."

"Vegas. Home ground." Harry's lips twisted wryly. "I thought you'd figured that one out, Lieutenant."

Konig wasn't amused. "We weren't the only ones who did," he warned. "Perhaps you'd like to hear what Ruskin's pulled together?"

Badr al-Hashid sat staring at the stone wall for a long time, waiting until the sounds from the adjacent homes stilled for the night. Rather than electric lighting, the flickering flame of an oil lamp illuminated the room. It cast shadows that moved against the wall with the grace and craft of a dancing girl, swaying sensuously, quivering winsomely.

There was no sign that the secret door had been disturbed since his last visit. Long ago he had christened the cache after an ancient mukarrib, a priest-ruler. The unifiers who had once guided the wealthy kingdoms of the Sabaeans.

Badr's lips curved in quiet satisfaction. Soon the acclaim which had eluded him for so long would be his. He would replace the plaque, covering any glaring signs of disturbance at the tomb, and seal it to await 'discovery', once the official papers were cleared by the government. Tedious details. The tedium of waiting. But he knew very well that without these precautions, the find would be sneered at by his colleagues.

The press would take notice. They would make his name as famous as that of Howard Carter. The uncovering of evidence that proved the existence of Bilqis, Queen of Sheba, would cast Tutankhamen into insignificance. What did a young Egyptian pharaoh matter, compared to a queen renowned in holy scripture?

He would schedule the discovery, make it public only when his father was far away on one of his trips to Somaliland. While Yussuf continued to search for new evidence of a link between the rich forests of frankincense in eastern Africa near Ethiopia, Badr would launch the most spectacular archaeological dig in history from his father's own home in Sirwah.

The golden plaque was encouraging. He had no way of knowing if the the tomb would contain items of such great value as were in King Tut's sepulcher. The pharaohs had taken items of great wealth on their journey across the River Styx. What would Bilqis's subjects have gathered in her honor? What wonders had passed through ancient Sheba from ports on the Gulf of Aden? Although the Red Sea separated western Arabia from its nearest neighbor, Egypt, ancient sea craft had been unable to weather the reefs and currents. Pirates had added to the dangers, threatening ships even when they traveled in ponderous fleets for protection. Ancient sea craft had been tiny and frail, built with flat bottoms. Far from seaworthy, they had kept to the coastlines. More daring merchants traveled from India and the Far East, bringing goods to the ports grouped at the lower edge of the Red Sea. It was from these prosperous towns that the caravan trails began and wound their way north to the Mediterranean ports. From there goods had dispersed outward to many ancient empires.

For centuries the caravans had traced the same routes, trusting to the monarchs and territorial Bedouin sheiks for protection. Based merely on the findings at Marib, the capital of Saba, the early Arabians had build a comfortable lifestyle, constructing a marvelously efficient dam across the Wadi Dhana. Today it was still possible to see the careful structure, to see the northern sluices, the overflow and the entrance to the long canal and additional manmade courses. When the monsoons brought rain to the mountains, the water that filled the *wadi* still followed those ancient courses. And Badr himself now awaited his moment of glory in the ancient fortress city of Sirwah to the south of Marib Dam.

The city quieted for the night around him. At long last, Badr moved to the seemingly solid stone wall. He pushed gently but forcefully on the right-hand side of a particular block. It gave slightly, then slid back to reveal the dark cavity. The feeble light shed by the flaring lamp wick made it appear even deeper and more dank. Badr's fingers found the edges of the hidden plaque and drew it forth. He sat back on his heels unmindful of the dust that stained his knees. His father hadn't used the house for over a month now. The mountain breeze had crept beneath the door, insinuated itself through cracks in the shutters, to deposit a fine grainy film of sand in every room. It was only disturbed where footsteps marked Badr's passage.

There was nothing dim or dingy about the plaque in his hands though. It had lain hidden for three thousand years but it glittered as brightly as though the craftsman who'd carved the inscription had just finished his work. Work that honored a queen.

Bilqis.

The name jumped out at him, seeming to separate itself from the other geometric shapes that made up the script. Bilqis. Badr sighed the name with all the ardor of a lover. Reverently, his finger followed the symbols.

Soon, my queen, he promised. *Soon.*

Chapter Thirteen

VALENTINA STRETCHED LAZILY and snuggled closer to Harry's side. He slept on, a contented half smile on his handsome face. Even in his sleep, his arm curved possessively over her ribs, one hand cupping her breast.

Heaven. It was pure heaven. Just as it had always been with Harry. She'd been a fool ever to desert him. Part of her had known it five years ago. She'd beat the nagging thought down, bludgeoning it into silence. She'd stored away the memories, pushing them far back in her mind, refusing to admit she'd been wrong.

Would it have made a difference if she'd stayed, back then? Harry'd been about to graduate and the job offers he'd had would have taken him far away from her. To follow him would have meant pushing her dreams aside, forgetting that she wanted her own specialized career in archaeology.

So what had she done? She'd thrown it all away. Everything. Her dreams, her aspirations, and Harry. The sight of another woman on his lap, her arms around his neck, her lips plastered to his, had made Valentina a little crazy.

A little? Valentina grimaced at the thought, and turned gently within the comfort of Harry's arms so that she could study his face.

She'd been afraid. Too young to know that Harry had not been encouraging the student in his lap. His arms weren't around the woman. His hands were on her wrists trying to pull her free. In retrospect Valentina had to admit, Harry hadn't acted like a man enjoying himself. He bolted out of the chair, nearly dumping the girl on the floor. But Valentina hadn't waited for an explanation. She was afraid it would be an apology she heard. Instead she sped home to the tiny apartment they shared. And she waited.

He didn't come home. Didn't call.

At first she cried, heart-rending sobs that shook her slim frame. Harry hadn't been there to comfort her. No one had. After the pain came a cold fury that withered, then killed every emotion she'd felt since witnessing that surprising tableau. She hadn't thought ahead, just acted. By dawn, her bags were already packed. The taxi dropped her at McCarran International Airport while the sun was still leaning sleepily against the peak of Sunrise Mountain. She was in Washington, D.C., in time for dinner. The next day she applied for her first secretarial position, in the office of one of her grandfather's friends. Her new life had begun.

A quiet, uneventful life.

Her grandparents accepted her explanation of missing them, of not finding school as exciting or interesting anymore. They merely assured her that if she changed her mind, she could always return to the university. Since her grandparents knew nothing of Harry's existence, or of her feelings for him, it was easy for Valentina to fall into the routine of their life. She already knew most of their friends. The new people she met were all part of the world of politics. There was nothing to remind her of archaeology, geology, or the bittersweet life she'd shared with Harry Smith.

Nothing except the dreams, that is. And after a while, even her subconscious left her in peace.

For four and a half years she'd endured the monotony of each day. Then she met Todd McAllister. He was the antithesis of Harry in looks and personality. There was nothing exciting or original in anything Todd did or said. His fair hair was always immaculate, never tousled. His gray eyes always seemed to radiate concern, dependability. "You look nice, Valentina," was the closest he ever came to a compliment. His expression had a limited number of variations, from mildly confused but genial, to deeply interested but bewildered. Todd always found a safe middle ground in any conversation. His stands were always pat, never vehemently for or against anything.

Valentina traced the beloved outline of Harry's face. His thick, black-brown hair stood in strangely attractive tufts. One batch, stubbornly refusing to follow the rest, peaked forward from his temple almost like a devilish horn. His jaw was darkly bristled, the shadows making the sculptured shape of his lips appear classical, timeless, like those of an ancient Greek sculpture of Apollo. Of course a work of art probably wouldn't be given such a hawkish looking nose. Nor would it have possessed as beautifully colored eyes. His long lashes sheltered them now, but Valentina knew when he woke she'd get lost once more in them, those perfect reflections of the clear desert sky.

Todd was an attractive man, too, but he'd never done more than give her chaste kisses. His thoughts had always been on avoiding any breath of scandal between himself and a former Senator's granddaughter. Harry had no such hesitation. He'd claimed not only her body but her soul with an intense fervency that Valentina found far better for her ego than all Todd's caution.

How could she ever have even contemplated becoming Todd McAllister's bride? What had once seemed so sensible, was now unthinkable.

As if her touch tickled, Harry's nose twitched. His eyelashes fluttered. The lovely blue of his eyes grew warm as they focused on her. His lips curved in lazy pleasure.

"Morning, gorgeous," he murmured huskily.

Valentina answered with a throaty growl and began the mating ritual she'd been foolish enough to abandon all those long years ago.

The motel was located just off the Strip, that gaudy length of Las Vegas Boulevard that stretches from the rather sedate-looking Sahara Hotel down past the newly opened Excalibur, with its drawbridge and representations of medieval turrets. In the five years that she'd been gone there had been a lot of changes. Not only the Excalibur had been added, but the owner of the Golden Nugget had built and opened a new hotel to sellout crowds. Harry promised they'd take time out to play tourist, visiting the lovely gardens at Steve Wynn's Mirage to watch the volcano erupt, and then see the white tigers that advertised Siegfied and Roy's extravaganza in the showroom. Or perhaps they'd attend the jousting tournament and medieval banquet at the Excalibur. Or, better yet, just go back to each of their favorite places—the top of the Mint downtown; the midway at Circus Circus; Cleopatra's Barge at Caesar's Palace. They could sample the buffet at the Golden Nugget, wander from place to place until it was time for the after midnight breakfast specials at Palace Station.

They spent a lazy morning in bed. Catching up on sleep lost during the hectic days of driving. Cathing up on lost years. Harry placed a call to Washington but the officer on duty had not been able to tell them anything new. So at long last Valentina and Harry dragged themselves to a Denny's Restaurant on the Strip for a quick brunch.

Valentina cuddled next to Harry in the booth, loath to be far from him. Beneath the table their thighs rested snugly against one another. She had chosen to wear a pair of new jeans today. Her knees were a bit sunburned from two days exposure to the sun. Her nose was trying to peel. But her cheeks were bright and her appetite continued to be healthy. Perhaps, she thought fondly, that was because sleeping with Harry again ensured her of a lot of very pleasant exercise. Valentina chose French toast and was generous with the syrup. Just to keep her energy level high in the event that the sightseeing was delayed yet again.

Harry's brow was creased in thought. From the uneventful long distance call? Valentina decided to find out.

"No word could be construed as good in our case, couldn't it?" she asked. The question was a bit muffled and unclear because her mouth was full, but Harry understood.

He cut into his Eggs Benedict. "Maybe. I wish Konig or Ruskin had been in. This is the first time I've called Washington that one of them wasn't on duty, though. If they had news for us, I'm sure that they would have left word. We'll stay put here for a few days in any event." The euphoria he'd felt when the Denver airport security guards had closed in on the Yemeni assassin had faded much too fast. Harry was pleased they'd acted on his tip about the man but his thoughts strayed often to the other news Konig had related the day before. Information he'd withheld from Valentina.

Her arm brushed his as Valentina reached for her orange juice. "When is the ball game?" she asked.

Harry paused, his fork half-way to his mouth. "You think that's the only reason we came to Vegas, don't you?"

Valentina drained the juice glass. Her eyes danced with mischief. She swirled her laden fork around on the plate, recoating a piece of French toast. "Didn't we?"

"Brat," he said fondly. "We're on our own ground here, Val. We know our way around. We've got friends to call on."

"A bunch of geologists?" She sounded skeptical but that could have been because she was licking a drop of syrup from the corner of her mouth at the same time.

"Nope. Denny decided to join the fire department rather than do road surveys. Gene opted for a fortune in real estate. He's been top salesman four times this last year."

"And now you're going to become an archaeologist. There's gonna be a real dearth of geologists at this rate," Valentina commented. Denny Northrup, a big shouldered, nearly neckless giant, had sandy hair, brown, cow eyes, and a ready laugh. Gene Beyer ran a close second in the popularity contest. He was nearly a head shorter than Denny and slight of build. Even at twenty-three he'd had a scholar's droop to his shoulders. His pale blond hair was fine and straight. Gene could talk a blue streak and loved the sound of his own voice. Back when she'd been part of the clique, Denny had been dating a long-legged dance major; Gene had just moved in with a petite student in the College of Hotel Administration.

"Are either of them still seeing Blythe or Nina?"' she asked.

Harry chuckled. "Far too much of them if you listen to Denny or Gene. They married the girls."

Valentina played with her empty orange juice glass. "Did you dance at their weddings?"

"At both. And with everyone." He grinned in remembrance. "Not that I remember much about either reception, other than the hangover I had the day after. Blythe and Nina have assured me the bridesmaids were always relieved when I passed out." He had no intention of telling her how much it had hurt to watch his best friends win the women of their choice when Valentina had run away from him. It hadn't been in celebration that he'd tipped a few too many glasses of champagne, it had been to dull the pain.

"Blythe gave up dancing for awhile, but now that the baby is nearly three, she's begun to answer audition calls again," Harry said. "Nina has been with Hilton for four years but wants to wangle a spot with

MGM when they open the theme park on the Strip in a couple years."

Valentina felt a bit stunned. Everyone else had gone on with their lives while she'd stagnated. "Denny and Blythe have a baby?" she repeated in astonishment.

Harry nodded and added sugar to his coffee. "Nina's expecting, too. They wrote ordering me to be back in the States in time to be godfather this time. I was in Australia when Phoenix was born."

Valentina nearly choked on her food. "Phoenix? Denny didn't really name his ... his ... what? Son? Daughter?"

"Daughter. Phoenix Northrup." Harry laughed at Valentina's expression. "Blythe's idea," he added. Rather needlessly, Valentina felt.

"Nina's not as ... er ... imaginative, is she? I mean, I'm speaking from personal experience, Harry," she explained. "Being named Valentina just because I was born on Valentine's Day, hasn't been easy."

Harry finished his breakfast and leaned back. "It's a beautiful name, Val. It suits you."

"So would Courtney."

"Not nearly as well," he murmured lovingly. "Valentina."

Maybe it wasn't so bad a name after all. Harry made each syllable throb exotically when he said it.

"What do you want to do today?" he asked.

She didn't have to think about it. "Library," she said. "I want to know more about the kind of artifact Badr might have found and where the kingdom of Sheba was located."

"Saba. Look for Saba," Harry corrected. "I'm not sure how much you'll find. The anthropology department at the U doesn't have an Arabian specialist that I know of. The pickin's might be lean."

Valentina grinned fondly at him. "But the Dickinson Library at the University is going to have a better selection than any of the Clark County branches. Did you plan to rent a car again or are we depending on cabs now?"

Harry stretch his long legs beneath the table a moment then finished off his coffee. "Why don't you take a cab? While you're gone I'll get a vehicle, maybe make reservations for a show tonight. What'll it be? The Lido? The Follies? Music? Comedy? Or magic and illusion with Siegfied and Roy?"

Just being with Harry was magic, Valentina thought. She had no illusions. It always had been, it always would be. "Make it a surprise." She paused and tapped a finger thoughtfully against her front teeth. "Of course, I don't have anything to wear," she pointed out. "We'll have to go shopping."

Harry grimaced melodramatically. "Let's change that to a movie at the Red Rock and a bucket of Kentucky Fried Chicken." He arranged to meet her back at their motel room at four o'clock. Valentina hurried away, her thoughts already turned back to the mystery of ancient artifacts. What, she wondered, would pottery from Sheba's era look like?

The campus of the University of Nevada at Las Vegas looked nearly the same as Valentina had remembered, though a number of new buildings had been added. Once it had been a commuter college with nearly all students living in the apartment buildings that ringed the campus. Now there were dorms, long multi-storied pink buildings that flanked one side of the parking lot of Thomas and Mack, the large, round basketball arena.

The taxi cab whipped off Tropicana and on to Maryland Parkway on the tail end of the caution arrow. "You plannin' on enrolling at UNLV?" the driver asked. "One of the fastest growin' universities in the country, ya know. My niece goes here. Gonna teach brats in junior high. I tell her, the way kids act today, you gotta have a class in how to handle a whip and chair." He chuckled, although Valentina was sure he'd told the same story to numerous passengers.

"No. I used to go here," she explained.

"Then I bet you were glued to your TV set during the finals last spring."

When she looked blank, the driver hastened to explain. "Basketball. When the Runnin' Rebels swooped up the championship. National champs. Geez, lady, this town went nuts."

"Oh, yes, of course," Valentina agreed quickly. She was glad that they were too close to her destination for him to go into a play-by-play commentary. Todd was not interested in sports other than tennis, so she hadn't followed college basketball. She knew what he meant, though, about the reaction of Las Vegans to a win. It might be an adult Disneyland to visitors, but at heart, Las Vegas was nothing more than a college town—a very proud college town.

The cabbie dropped her at the student union so he could follow

146

the loop back out to the street on his way to a fare at McCarran International Airport or back on the Strip. For old times sake, Valentina went inside and bought a coke at the snackbar. She wandered into the bookstore and came out with matching sweat shirts for Harry and herself, both broadcasting the national basketball win. As an alumnus, Harry would enjoy it. He'd never missed a Rebels game when they'd been together. One season he'd even tried to shape his thick dark mustache into a flowing handlebar like the one worn by the little Yosemite Sam character, the Runnin' Rebel. The sweat shirts she'd bought showed the stocky reb riding a bucking, evilly grinning shark, the second team mascot, designed to honor their controversial basketball coach, Jerry Tarkanian.

Although a new alumni building was just being completed, and the new Howard Hughes College of Engineering building now covered what had once been frisbee playing ground, the James Dickinson Library looked the same—as odd as ever. Two buildings had been joined to expand the library's square footage. One was round, and, in what seemed an illogical move, it held the bulk of the collected volumes. The addition was an uninspired rectangle four stories tall. Valentina had heard it compared to a stack of mobile homes. A two-story bright-red tube connected the fairly incompatible buildings at the second and third floor layers.

The on-line catalogue was new since her day, but it only took a few tries before she got the hang of calling up information on the computer. Within ten minutes she was in the stacks dragging out books on Yemen and Arabian archaeological excavations.

The photographs in the books reminded her sharply of the artifacts she had seen on exhibit in Washington. Had it just been last Friday night? It was only Wednesday but she felt as if weeks had gone by. Too much had been happening. Getting shot at. Having a dead man in the living room. Being on the run. Being with Harry. She'd started this adventure with a lot of emotional baggage from the past. Now she was looking forward to the future, one she'd share not with a staid politician, but with a charming rogue, a geologist turned archaeologist.

She must remember to ask Harry which school he planned to get his doctorate from so that she could enroll as well. Why be the only member of the Bakil family who wasn't an archaeologist? The thought brought a smile to her face which had nothing to do with the lovely frieze of stylized ibexes on the page before her. If Dawud, Badr, and Harry ever got together, she'd probably never get a word in edgewise if she didn't find a field of her own to babble about. And there was much more to pottery than just microscopic mineral particles. The shapes, the colors, the painted designs, the craftsmanship ...

Valentina forced her mind away from contemplation of the future and settled down to her research.

Before long she realized that, in trying to single out information about Bilqis, Badr al-Hashid had had his hands extremely full. Saba hadn't been the only kingdom in the area. He'd dealt with the written languages of obscure civilizations: the Minaeans, Qatabanians, and Hadramaut. But she found what seemed to be a further link to Solomon. The written dialect of the Sabaeans had features in common with those of northern Arabia. That could be construed as the area near Solomon's court in Judea.

The inscriptions shown in her reference book were geometric in design and look. They were nothing like the lovely flowing Arabic hand of modern scholars. Not only had the script changed drastically, there were ongoing modifications through the early centuries. Some, the author claimed, with little or no indication of a gradual shift in form.

As fascinating as the information was, it wasn't getting Valentina any closer to knowing what she needed. She flipped pages more quickly, skimming for content.

She thought about the artifact Badr had recovered, possibly from a thief, and hidden in the secret cache that Harry's half of the map indicated. It seemed logical to suppose that it wasn't merely an ordinary tablet detailing taxes or other daily business in the kingdom. The only things that would have gotten Badr overly excited would have been something more personal. Like a palace. Or more specifically, the queen's own tomb.

Tombs were full of personal artifacts, articles that had been used daily by the deceased. Valentina recalled from her own studies on the American Indian Basketmaker cultures, that the earliest people had lived in pit houses. The dug-out homes had merely been filled in when the owner died, becoming his burial spot, complete with household goods and food stuffs. Archaeologists had been able to piece together a picture of their lives from the evidence in the tombs.

The same academic reconstruction would be done in Yemen, if Badr indeed knew the location of Bilqis's last resting place. Would the find detail more than just the life of a wealthy woman? Would it lend credence to the stories of Solomon as well?

Valentina slowed. The word *tomb* nearly jumped off the page at her.

The only excavated cave tombs in Yemen had been located in the scree slopes edging the *wadi*, the often dry water courses that wove out of the mountains. Although they had been nothing more than ossuaries, places where the bones of the dead were collected, Valentina found another fact very attractive. The author felt that the tombs had been connected to a temple located near the main *wadi*.

Valentina sat back in her chair and stared at the ceiling. Around her, students involved in summer session classes stretched and frowned at their books. One young man ran his hands through sun-bleached hair and then stretched, arching his back and rippling his biceps. The girl across the table looked a bit dazed, then interested. He didn't notice her though and soon both students were studying once more.

Valentina chewed her lip in thought. If these smaller, rather unexciting tombs had been near a temple, wouldn't the grave of a queen be in or near a temple? In Europe, medieval monarchs had been buried in churches. In ancient Egypt they'd carted them off to the spectacular Valley of the Kings, or built pyramids. What would the Sabaeans have done for Bilqis?

She thought back over the things Harry had told her. Not just about Badr's obsession but about their childhood adventures. One of those imaginary games had turned into a game of murder now.

A temple. She was sure Harry'd said something about a temple. Something about living in a mountain city because it was near the excavation site. Where had that been? What had the excavation been?

Valentina dragged a macro-encyclopedia to her table and then an atlas. With half a dozen books spread out around her, she plotted a course.

San'a' sat nearly in the center of the northern section of Yemen. Marib was to the east, closer to the stretching sand fingers of the giant Rub' Al-Khali Desert. With the help of the descriptions in the book on excavations, Valentina located Sirwah, just to the south of

Marib. In her favorite of the books, page after page of photographs showed the standing pillars and crumbling walls of structures in the heart of the ancient capital.

"The great wall of the temple of 'Ilumquh at Sirwah with its fine ashlar masonry and a dedication to the deities," the caption under one photo read. Valentina held her breath a moment and leafed back a few pages. "The national god of each of the kingdoms or states was the Moon-god known by various names: 'Ilumquh ... 'Awwam ..." More pages turned. "The most famous open temple was that of 'Awwam situated near Marib ..." Valentina read on.

Perhaps they weren't big enough pieces to complete the puzzle, but the picture was filling in. Badr and Harry had grown up in the shadow of the ruins at Marib, ruins that stretched to the neighboring town of Sirwah in which they lived. Both Sirwah and Marib had been on the caravan route, a trail that lead from the Gulf of Aden north to the prosperous countries that lined the Mediterranean Sea. According to legend, Bilqis, Queen of Sheba/Saba, had traveled north. Both the Bible and the Koran recorded a visit of a Queen of Sheba to Solomon's court. Solmon had worshipped one God, a God known through history by many names: Yahweh, Jehovah, Allah. But the temple outside of Sirwah was dedicated to the Moon-god, 'Ilumquh or 'Awwam.

Valentina chewed on a fingernail thoughtfully. If Bilqis's tomb was indeed within reach, it seemed very likely that scholars had been overlooking it for over a century. It had to be near Sirwah, near the excavated Temple of 'Awwam. It was equally illogical for Bilqis's subjects to have placed her tomb along the scree sides of the *wadi*. After the monsoons had passed through, the water could have risen sufficiently to tear away at the opening of the burial. Therefore it had to be on higher ground.

Would the queen's tomb provide proof that she had journeyed to Solomon's court? Would there be an artifact proclaiming the glory of Yahweh rather than that of 'Awwam? If so, it might be a clue to why her name hadn't been written down, why she had become nothing more than a legend. After all, the Egyptians had tried to eradicate any memory of Amenhotep IV, Akhenaton, after his death. He had been the only pharaoh to attempt to turn his people to the worhip of one god, although it had been Aton the sun god, if

Valentina remembered her Egyptology correctly. Aton had at least been one of the Egyptian gods. What would happen to a monarch who attempted to turn her subjects to the worship of not just one god, but to a foreign god? Bilqis couldn't have learned a lesson from the man who had preceded King Tut on the throne. She'd lived hundreds of years after Akhenaton tempted fate, but there was a good chance she had never heard of him. Her world was narrow, bounded by the desert, the mountains, and the small glimpse she received of the outside world through travelers along the caravan route.

It didn't matter that Bilqis's name didn't figure in the daily business transactions of her neighboring nations. The Hittites, Sumerians, Assyrians, Babylonians, and Egyptians had been far larger nations compared to her Saba. They were the giants of the ancient world. Even Solomon's kingdom had been small by comparison. Why should empires bother to mention a queen who ruled a small area along the caravan trail?

Valentina picked up the volume that dealt with excavations in southern Arabia and headed for the vending machines in the library lobby. When she had taken a few cold gulps of coke and made inroads on a Milky Way, she opened the book once more.

Despite all she'd learned and the suppositions she'd made, Valentina still didn't feel she had discovered why anyone would attack both Harry and Badr. Each attempt had been upon their life. Just to gain a scrap of paper drawn by a couple of boys?

She'd never actually heard of a case where an academic had killed an associate over a find. Where one made a name for himself with a discovery, another could always become equally famous by ripping apart every theory, premise, and thesis his colleague broached. What men killed for was money. Lots of money.

From the photographs of the artifacts at the Marib and Sirwah sites, it didn't look as if the kingdom of Saba had been that wealthy. Perhaps there was a further hint in the book though.

It wasn't exactly 10th century B.C. stuff, but there was a little more information about the Sabaeans. A Greek had written of them: "The chief city of this tribe is called by them Sabae ... surpasses not only the neighboring Arabs but also all other men in wealth and in their several extravagances ..."

Hmm. Valentina pondered a moment then shook her head.

Although the Greek civilization had been on the rise, it hadn't been ready to fling out men who wrote travelogues yet. It didn't sound like the same era in which either Solomon or Sheba had reigned.

Still she read on. Embossed goblets of silver and gold, couches with silver feet, gilded bed columns, silver figures, coffers made of gold and set with precious stones. A high standard of workmanship had prevailed and the use of materials of natural beauty: gold, bronze, alabaster. Proficient craftsmen had created figurines of bronze, jewelry of gold and semi-precious stones, designed coins. Varying types of design and manufacture had issued from kilns ...

Reluctantly Valentina pulled herself away. No one would kill for pottery. She had to keep her mind on items that were of value outside of their historical significance. The more she learned, the less inclined she was to believe the person who was behind the murderous attempts on both Harry and Badr knew anything about the era in which Bilqis had lived. There was no evidence or legend to indicate that the Queen of Sheba had collected riches to compare with those of the legendary coffers of King Solomon.

In one last effort, Valentina flicked through the pages of her reference book. The last of the Milky Way disappeared.

What she found only confirmed her opinion. Burials had been varied but really nothing more than "stone-lined graves covered with a cairn of stones, excavated tombs in the scree slopes at the side of *wadis* with concealed entrances, and mausolea with chambers ..." Ah! Valentina leaned forward eagerly over the table. "Having a belief in an after-life, the dead were usually buried with material objects which they had required during life. These included jewelry, pottery and alabaster vessels, stelae, money and figurines."

Valentina closed the book and kissed the cover. "Thank you, Gus!" she murmured. Then she left *Hajar Bin Humeid: Investigations at a Pre-Islamic Site in South Arabia* by Gus W. Van Beek on the table and flew out the door. It was long past four o'clock now. Harry would be waiting for her. She was anxious to hear how he answered her question. Because if Badr's wife really had no concept of the type of artifacts to be found in Bilqis's tomb, then Valentina was sure she knew who had tried to kill Harry.

He'd been right all along, of course. His cousin Sikina was a very dangerous lady.

Chapter Fourteen

HARRY LAY STRETCHED out on the bed, hands behind his head, contemplating the nice curve the fates had thrown him. Imagine. He smiled at the ceiling. After five years Valentina had become a special part of his life again. And she would become even more precious when she became his wife.

He wasn't going to give her much time to think her way out this time. They were in Nevada, the land of quick marriages. Their nuptuals would even be performed with family there to bless the union, for Loretta Crosby was on her way to Las Vegas. He'd been a little disconcerted when Konig had relayed the information. Loretta had asked that the Washington police pass along the news adding that she had a pleasant surprise for both Harry and Valentina. Harry hadn't the foggiest idea what that might be, but he'd felt life would be less fraught if he withheld that tidbit from Valentina.

In the short span of a few days she had become the girl he'd wooed and won long ago. He doubted McAllister would even recognize her now. Her eyes were brighter. Her clothes were more startling than sophisticated. And she was nearly always hungry. It wouldn't be long before the weight she'd lost was back, filling out her cheeks, softening the sharp angles of her figure.

A glance at his watch showed that it was nearly four o'clock. She'd be there soon. Harry enjoyed picturing Valentina's reaction to the car he'd rented. A candy-apple red Corvette. Not exactly the vehicle of a man who was trying to hide, but then he wasn't running any more. He'd turned, braced, ready to face down Sikina and her minions.

The slip of paper with the phone numbers of both Denny Northrup and Gene Beyer lay on the night stand next to the phone. He'd call them later, or tomorrow. Perhaps during the day, so he'd catch their answering machines while they were at work. Then he could let them know he'd arrived but still have plenty of time alone with Valentina. Of course with Denny's schedule at the fire department there was no telling when he'd be home. All those twenty-four-hour long days on the job followed by a succession of days off duty at home. It hadn't just been the excitement and danger that had lured Northrup to the job. He'd always been the laziest lout Harry knew. Gene, on the other hand, probably had given him the number of his mobile phone. Beyer was a man who didn't know the meaning of the word *relaxation*. He was always on the go.

There was a quiet, tentative knock on the door. Harry rolled to his feet. His sunglasses fell out of his shirt pocket and Harry picked them up in an unconscious reflex action. He was always dropping them, losing them. It was getting harder to find mirrored lenses, too. At least, ones he like. He'd paid one helluva lot for this pair. Of course, Valentina would be delighted if they were broken. She'd always hated them. Insisted he acted as if his sunglasses were sacred religious relics. In a way maybe they were. They always reminded him of Val and her slow-burning temper. Over the last five years they'd been a talisman to him.

The tap sounded on the door again. Sunglasses still in his hand, Harry pulled it open expecting to see Valentina's bright smile, to hear her bubbling with information about the sites at Marib and Sirwah.

It was the second time in less than a week that he'd opened the door to a man with a gun.

"Hadi," his cousin, Sikina, cooed softly. She stood next to the man, offside from the weapon, sheltering it from the sight of others. The last time he'd seen her, Sikina had been draped in the dark, flowing robes of an Islamic woman. Not all women followed the old regime, but Badr had been a stickler who insisted his wife cover herself. Perhaps he had good reason. Sikina was a very lovely woman.

154

Dressed now in a short, clinging western dress, Sikina was ravishing.

Harry didn't bother to act surprised. "I knew you wouldn't be far behind me when I recognized the man in Denver," he said and stepped back.

The man with the gun moved into the room. Sikina followed, closing the door behind her.

"Sattam? Did you kill him, Hadi?" She didn't sound the least concerned about her henchman.

"Disabled him," Harry said. "He's still alive, *bint 'amm bannaat*, cousin. It makes it so much easier for him to implicate you in attempted murder."

Sikina slinked over to the window. She held one edge of the heavy blackout drape to the side, enabling her to see the parking lot.

To see Valentina's imminent arrival.

Harry's mouth went dry.

"Where is it, Hadi?" Sikina asked. Her voice was quite calm. She was as cool as if she was in her own home back in San'a' asking if he cared for another cup of thick, sweet Turkish coffee.

"Where is what? The treasure? I don't know."

The man snarled something. His accent was beyond Harry's comprehension but he wasn't keen on having Sikina translate the phrase for him.

Sikina turned slightly. With the sunlight at her back, her profile was shadowed. Her smile wasn't particularly pleasant though. "The Treasure of the Unifier? Of course you know, Hadi. I saw you draw the map. I saw you tear it in half and give Badr the insignificant side."

"We were children then. The treasure was never anything more than my baseball gear. You remember how the other children always wanted to finger my stuff."

Sikina had turned back to the window. "I understand you are traveling with a woman," she said. "Is she very lovely, Hadi?"

This was not going well. "Who told you that? They were mistaken. I'm here alone."

"Still so gallant," Sikina purred. Valentina's shopping bag lay in the chair nearest the window. He'd forgotten about it. Sikina dipped her hand within it, rustling sacks to draw forth a delicate flesh colored lace edged teddy. "All I want is the map," Sikina said and dropped the lingerie back in the bag. "You can give it to me now. Or we can wait for your woman to return."

He tried another track. "The map?" Harry laughed lightly. "Ah, Sikina. '*Asal*, it was lost long ago. Why would I keep a child's toy?"

"To regain your treasure."

"A baseball mitt? I grew up and bought a new one." Harry played with one hinge of his sunglasses, moving the earpiece back and forth absently. Surreptitiously, he glanced at his watch. After four. Valentina could arrive at any moment. "You can have the glove and ball I left in Sirwah, Sikina," he offered. "Ask Badr to show you where the cache is. He doesn't need a map to find it."

His cousin's slim back had stiffened. What had she seen? Surely not Val, Harry argued silently. Although he'd carried her picture with him, Sikina had never to his knowledge seen it. But she'd definitely seen something that had scared her. What? Or, rather, whom?

Sikina stepped back from the window and faced him. "Do not take me for a fool, Hadi. Even if you do not carry the map you know the location of the treasure. You will tell me how to find it." She motioned to the man with the gun. "We will take him with us," she snapped. *"Bi-sur'a.* Hurry."

The man made a protest, a low gutteral growl. Sikina snapped a sharp answer. Harry caught a name he hadn't heard before. A name that stood out because the syllables sang of a different drummer, of the muscial lilt of a different nation. *Faraday*.

He'd barely made a mental note of it before the gunman was manhandling him. Harry jerked his arm away, pretended to make a grab for the gun and dropped his sunglasses. While the Arab chortled at his victim's ineptitude, Harry dodged a blow and purposefully stepped on the glasses. The next blow was delivered with the butt of the gun. It hit Harry solidly on the back of the head, stunning him. While Sikina grated out instructions, the assassin draped Harry's arm around his shoulders and dragged him out the door.

Sikina gave one last look around the tidy motel room, then closed the door quietly behind her.

Valentina was longing for a shower. Of course it had been impossible to find a cab anywhere near the University. She'd considered calling for one, then changed her mind. It would have taken twenty minutes to half an hour or more for one to answer. They all hated to leave the airport or the Strip where fares were more frequent and the tips healthier. She wasn't that far from the motel. She'd walk.

It wasn't the two or three miles that wore her out. It was the temperature. In the years she'd been gone, she'd lost the acclimation that made exercise possible under a sun that turned the concrete into a sizzling griddle. Even the Big Gulp she'd bought hadn't helped much.

The motel was in sight now. She'd fall in the door, collapse on the bed with the air conditioning turned on full blast. Once she revived, the shower would continue the rehabilitation. Idly she wondered what movies were playing at the Red Rock Theatres. She and Harry would sit in the last row. Maybe they'd even pay attention to the film.

She stumbled up to the door and tried the knob. It didn't move. Valentina knocked impatiently. Then she knocked harder. She looked at her watch. It was nearly five. Where the hell was Harry?

Fury gave her the strength to backtrack to the office to ask for a second key. The door had barely swung closed behind her when Valentina heard a man call her by name.

Her heart jumped in terror before she realized she knew that voice. "Oh, Sergeant Ruskin" she breathed. "What are you doing here?"

He smiled. It was a quiet grin. The edges of his eyes crinkled softly. He looked almost apologetic. "Looking for you," Ruskin said.

"Me?" Her eyes widened. "Oh, my gosh! Something's happened to Grandma!"

"No, no. She's fine. It's Smith I'm worried about."

"Smith." She growled the name. "He's dead when I find him. He was supposed to be here at four. Now I'm locked out and he's God knows where."

The clerk behind the desk looked up from her papers. "Are you talking about Mr. Harry Smith?" she asked. "He was here about a quarter to four to give us the license number of his rental car. If it's still here, he should be in the room." She flipped through her file and then read a number off the card.

Ruskin stepped outside the door. Valentina followed him. The room was directly across from the office. It was easy to read the plates on the three cars lined up before that wing.

"A Corvette?" Valentina's voice cracked. "A red Vette? Oh, God. Harry." She turned to Ruskin, her eyes now wide with fear. "He made it too easy for them to find him! He sent me off and ..."

"We don't know that," Ruskin said quickly. In short order he retrieved a second key from the desk and led a shaky Valentina across the lot. "You stay out here a moment while I check," he said firmly, as he unlocked the door. His hand automatically reached for the gun he was no longer carrying. Officially, Konig had insisted, he was on vacation. He was out of his jurisdiction. Really far out of it. So the revolver stayed in his locker at the police station while he followed this strange case to its conclusion.

Valentina didn't follow his instructions, of course. He hadn't really expected her to. This was the girl who had thrown herself down a flight of stairs to face two killers. She'd done so with a gun she knew to be empty. No, she'd never comply with any directions that went contrary to what her feelings for Harry Smith told her to do. At least she stayed just inside the door while Ruskin checked the alcove and the bathroom. As expected, the room was empty.

Valentina sank down on the end of the bed. "Where is he?" she asked in a small, fearful voice. "Did she follow us here?"

"She?" Ruskin paused in his search. No signs of a struggle. The only evidence that the room had been used that day were the pillows piled against the headboard of the bed. They were still indented where Smith had leaned against them. The keys to both the rented Corvette and the room were still on the dresser. Two backpacks rested on the luggage rack but they didn't look as if they'd been searched. "What makes you think the person behind the attempts is a woman, Ms. Crosby?"

Valentina was still pale with fright. The sun-touched color of her nose and cheeks looked brighter against that pallor. Her eyes looked larger. They were dry though. And as hard as glittering green gemstones.

"Because no one else had the opportunity to know about things," she said. "We figured out that the map Harry and Badr drew as children is important. They found a secret compartment in Badr's father's house in Yemen. And they made a game of it. Drew a map. Tore it in half. Harry kept his share for old times sake. Only three people knew about that map. Harry, Badr and Sikina."

"Sikina Hashid," Ruskin brought her name out with difficulty. "She's here in Vegas."

"Lord," Valentina breathed. "Then Harry's got to be with her now. Couldn't she just be content with the map? Did she have to take him away, too?"

Ruskin hesitated, then sat down on the bed next to Valentina. "Maybe she doesn't have the map," he suggested. "Tell me more about it. Why is it so important? Is there really a treasure hidden in this niche?"

Valentina nodded. "We think so. You see, Harry thinks that Badr has ... er ... acquired an artifact that might lead to a major archaeological find. We think it's hidden in the cache." She paused. "What makes you think they don't have the map?"

Ruskin shrugged. "Guess work. A hunch. Where had Smith kept it?"

"Up until a couple of days ago? In his wallet. But we hid it among the rest of our road maps. You know, the old *Purloined Letter* trick."

"Do you still have the maps?"

Valentina was already halfway to the waiting backpacks. "I think so," she said. The first bag held her own clothing. Valentina barely glanced through it. She found what she wanted in Harry's. It took a few minutes of unfolding each accordian map before the scrap fell out.

Settled once more next to Ruskin, Valentina launched into her explanation. She told him of Badr's reputation, of Sikina's strange upbringing with its dangerous sampling of Western life and of her sister's marriage to an American. From there she launched into the facts she'd gathered at the library. "So you see, Sergeant, the little bit Sikina knows is dangerous. She doesn't realize that what Badr would consider a treasure beyond measure wouldn't add up to the price of a decent meal at a gourmet restaurant. Sure there are collectors out there who'd pay for stone slates, three-thousand-year-old pots, and alabaster statuettes. But she thinks the find is something like King Tut's tomb; gold, silver, precious jewels. She probably pictures chests full of the stuff, like in a pirate movie. For that she's willing to kill."

"And you think she has a partner in Arabia, who is either from Europe or America?"

"Harry claims no Arab man would let her have this long a leash," Valentina insisted.

Ruskin ran a hand over the back of his neck seeking to ease the tension. Put together with the facts he'd gathered, the theory fit awfully well—even when he put aside his own smarting ego. Sikina had used him and Ruskin didn't like that.

"Are we sure that Smith didn't just walk off to the nearest casino?" he asked. "It's easy to lose track of time when you're involved in a game of chance."

Valentina chewed her bottom lip. "No, I'm not sure," she admitted. "But I am sure that if he was being taken away against his will, Harry would have left a sign: something that they wouldn't notice in the event they straightened the place up after the struggle."

Ruskin stood up. "Okay. We search."

But Valentina had already found the evidence. She bent to pick up the item she'd just kicked. The double reflection of her own worried face was broken now, shattered. Valentina cradled the mangled sunglasses between her hands. "Oh, she's got him alright," she said quietly.

Chapter Fifteen

BY SEVEN O'CLOCK the rescue squad was ensconced in Valentina's motel room. They'd brought pizza with them.

Denny Northrup was stretched out on the bed hogging all the pillows behind him as a backrest. His wife Blythe had tucked her long shapely legs into a lotus position next to him. Since Nina Beyer, eight months pregnant, had collapsed into the nearest chair, and Sergeant Cole Ruskin had taken the second chair, Valentina and Gene Beyer were left to fend as best they could at the end of the bed. It barely left room for the three large pizza boxes.

"So you think this Sikina is holding Harry somewhere in the city?" Denny asked before taking a huge bite of sausage, pepperoni, mushroom and olive with extra cheese.

"If you'd had the sense to become a policeman instead of a fireman you could probably find out where," Valentina said. She accepted the can of Coors that Gene passed her and popped the tab. "Poor Cole can't even ask for help since he's officially on vacation."

Ruskin smiled wearily. He'd become Cole to all of them the moment lithe, blond, beautiful Blythe had slithered in the door and recognized the admiration in his eyes. Northrup was used to men ogling his wife though. He'd just slapped the visiting police officer on the back. Just to be safe, Ruskin had chosen to keep the room between himself and Blythe.

"What we need," Ruskin said, "is a way to check rentals this week."

"And not apartment or efficiency rentals," Nina added. She stared unhappily at the glass of apple juice in her hand. Then longingly at the beers the others were drinking. "She'd have taken a house."

"How do you figure that?" Denny demanded. "Houses ain't cheap."

"She's not exactly on a budget," Nina said. "But that's not the reasoning she'd use. She'd take a house, my dears," she continued smugly, "because she has a servant with her."

It sounded so logical. "Lord, you're right." Valentina was stunned. "But that means we've got the mole we need."

"Mole?" Gene Beyer sounded put out. "God what kind of trash have you been reading, Val?"

"It wasn't anything personal," she assured him. "Can you do it though?"

"You betcha, sweet," Gene said. "I'll be right back."

When the door closed behind him, Denny's thick brow was creased in puzzlement. "Can he do what?"

"Pull up house rentals on the computer, of course. Harry said Gene was making his fortune in real estate now."

Blythe sighed in ecstasy. "Is he ever. You should see the house they just bought, Val. I'd kill for it. Five bedrooms, three with attached baths ..."

"We'll give you the grand tour," Nina said. "After we get Harry back."

Gene returned within minutes with a portable computer and modem. He shoved Northrup aside to set up next to the telephone. Before long he was connected to the system at his office. "Okay. What's her name again?"

Ruskin pulled his chair closer to view the screen. He spelled out Sikina's full name, the one she'd given him just a few days ago for his report. The address surfaced quickly.

Denny whistled softly. "Calico Basin. Not exactly close in, is she?"

Gene bit into a fresh slice of pizza, a thoughtful expression on his face. "Not easy to sneak up on either."

At Ruskin's querying look, Denny jumped in to explain. "Calico Basin is on the edge of Red Rock Canyon. Part of the national park system. Only a few homes out there, on multi-acre lots. No trees, not even many large rocks. Rolling hills, then cliff faces. I'm guessing she's taken the new place out there."

Gene picked up the story. "It's the perfect place to hide out in comfort," he agreed. "The house was built by some up and coming actor whose career stopped coming and started going. Downhill. Fast. Marriage broke up but they're still battling it out in the courts as to who gets the house. Until then, to make the mortgage payment, the house has been rented, short term, completely furnished to whoever can afford the asking price. It's maybe a half-hour, forty-five minute drive from here, straight west."

Ruskin studied both the men. "So we need a diversion, is that it?"

Denny thought about it a moment. "Yeah. As much as I'd prefer to go tonight, the terrain is unfamiliar. Morning would be a better assault time."

Valentina moved to peer over their shoulders at the screen of Beyer's portable computer. "Assault time? This isn't a game, Northrup. It's life and death. Harry's."

"A figure of speech, Val," Denny insisted. "If it will make you feel better, Cole here can run the whole operation."

Blythe unwound her legs and crawled over to join the group at the side of the bed. "Sorry, Val," she said. "Denny's been on a war movie kick lately."

"Like we couldn't tell," Gene grumbled. He jotted the address down, then eased out of the program. "I've got a suggestion." He looked straight at Cole Ruskin. " 'Course you might not like it."

Ruskin grinned. His eyes moved from one anxious face to another. From petite, dark Nina in her ballooning maternity garb and her fair, studious-looking mate, to ethereal Blythe and her linebacker-clone husband, to the serious, direct eyes of Valentina Crosby. Whatever this group of old friends planned, it probably wouldn't be legal. As part of it he could lose his job back in Washington, a job that would be on the line anyway, if anyone ever heard that he'd passed information to Sikina Hashid.

"I'm listening," he said.

The cream-colored Cadillac, its doors emblazoned with the insignia of a reputable real estate agency, pulled into the curving driveway, passed the pink Cupid who frolicked in the dry fountain, passed the uncompleted landscaping. The dapper man in the light-weight gray suit got out and tucked a clipboard beneath his arm. He slammed the car door but didn't bother to lock it. No one other than himself was there to notice that he'd also left the keys in the ignition in the event he felt a quick getaway was the next intelligent move. He strode to the double bleached-oak front doors of the long, white-stucco ranch house and leaned on the bell.

Around the house, cliffs rose sharply, tilting toward the rising sun. Their geological layers stood out in brilliant relief. Various shades of red, white, gray, brown, and yellow colored the landscape. It was the variety of colors in the rock that had given this canyon its name. It wasn't as gaudy as the national park directly to the west with its brighter shades of red, but the name Calico Basin definitely fit.

From her reclining position at the crest of the adjacent hill, Valentina Crosby squinted through binoculars to bring Gene Beyer into focus. The door was answered by a man who scowled darkly at the unexpected visitor. Then she got her first glimpse of Harry's cousin. Sikina's dark hair was bound in a neat chignon, her simple dress clung to voluptuous curves, her dark eyes and warm dusky skin were exotic. Valentina felt colorless and plain suddenly.

She passed the binoculars to Cole Ruskin. He lay next to her in the dirt. In worn jeans, sneakers, and a white T-shirt with the familiar golden circle logo of the Hard Rock Cafe (Washington, D.C.), he didn't look much like a police officer anymore.

"He's inside," Ruskin announced and passed the binoculars over Valentina's head to Denny Northrup, also sprawled in the dust. Northrup had an official's whistle dangling from a cord around his neck. His shirt was also white but it advertised a recent tour by rock and roller Robert Palmer.

"Remember, three sharp blasts when Beyer leaves," Ruskin told the fireman.

"Right." Denny looked at his watch. "You've got ten minutes until Blythe drives the jeep past. She'll wait for you on the dirt road that runs about a hundred feet behind the house. Just the other side of that ridge. It'll keep her hidden until you get out."

Valentina's eyes were large with fright but the set of her jaw was determined. "Okay. Are we ready then?"

Ruskin grinned. His blood was pumping as fast as water from a hydrant on a summer's day. "Yeah. It's time, Val."

She was up and over the hill, almost sliding down it in her eagerness. Together they edged around the house, moving away from the formal rooms where Gene Beyer held Sikina and, hopefully, her henchman a captive audience while he asked a long series of questions for a fictitious form. She followed Ruskin's every move, flattening herself against the side of the building while he peered in the windows. Only one room had the curtains drawn—two other rooms had shown evidence of use. This had to be it. Valentina bit her lip, holding her breath while Ruskin removed the screen and then cut a neat hole in the glass.

"Burglar's trick," he mouthed at her as he lifted the piece away and reached in to unlock the window.

The pane slid back with barely a sigh. Ruskin reached through and carefully pushed the curtain aside. He could see one end of a bed and a scuffed Nike shoe. "Bingo," he whispered.

Although the house was single story, the ground dropped away at the back before climbing up to a small ridge. Ruskin cupped his hands to give Valentina a boost to the window sill. He had to give her hips a further rather familiar shove before she got her foot on the ledge and could swing through the window. He pulled himself up behind her.

Valentina slid from behind the closed drapes and paused. A smile of amusement twitched her lips. "Never a camera when you need one," she murmured.

From his trussed position on the bed, Harry glared at her.

The bed had been equipped with both a headboard and footboard of gently curving brass. The bedspread was a design of delicate flowers, all pinks, powder blues, spring greens, and soft yellows.

Ruffles decorated the bolsters. Harry looked out of place in the feminine setting. Not just because of the pastel colors. More because of his ridiculous position.

Valentina had thought only heroines in melodramatic gothic romances got to be tied to the bedposts. But Sikina's henchman apparently hadn't read the same books. He had bound Harry in a spread-eagle position, hands and legs tied to opposite corners. A colorful washcloth had been stuffed in his mouth and bound in place with a tasseled drapery cord.

Moving quietly, Valentina crossed the room and curled up next to Harry. "Fiendish," she whispered and tugged at the gag. "They were trying to get the information by tickling you, weren't they?"

Harry made a noise deep in his throat. "Val," he croaked.

"Hush," she admonished. "Stay still while Cole cuts you loose."

"Cole?" His voice was barely a whisper but the suspicion was very clear.

Ruskin pushed back the curtains, flooding the room with light. "Rescue party," he said and opened a pocketknife. While Harry blinked in the blazing sunlight, Ruskin sawed away, freeing first the victim's hands, then his ankles. "Can you walk?"

Harry tried. His knees gave. "Sorry. Circulation's not back yet."

Ruskin frowned. "We can't wait. You support him on one side, Val."

They got Harry to the window. Valentina slid through as easily as if she'd been hopping through windows in a clandestine fashion all her life. Ruskin helped Harry, then joined them quickly.

Because the owners had never completed their landscaping, there was no pool to avoid or patio wall to jump. It was just as well. The pace the three of them set across the open stretch of desert wasn't as fast as any of them would have liked. They made dragging tracks across the dry dust. Once Harry tripped over a tuft of mesquite. Valentina stepped on a loose rock and had to be saved from sliding back down the slope into Sikina's rented back yard. Ruskin, fortunately, proved as sure-footed as a mountain goat.

They had reached the top of the hill when the warning blasts came from Denny's whistle. Down on the dirt road before them, Blythe yelled encouragement. She kept the engine of Denny's jeep running.

Behind them came a sharp command. Valentina glanced back to see the dark-featured man who worked for Sikina swing through the open window. Behind him, Harry's lovely cousin snapped orders, a very unlovely expression on her face.

"Shit," Ruskin swore. "Can you make it alone?"

Valentina had already bolted, trying to drag Harry with her. He slipped out of her grasp. "I owe this guy something," he hissed and stumbled back to where Ruskin had crouched down, just below the crest of the rise. "Go on, Val."

She had no intention of moving. He should have known she wouldn't take orders. Instead she hunched down in the scant cover of a larger mesquite bush. "Be careful," she urged.

Harry dropped down and scooped up a double handful of dirt. When the charging man came over the ridge, Harry threw it in his face. Ruskin followed by tripping the temporarily blinded man. He slid face forward down the hill. Before the kidnapper could get to his feet, Harry and Ruskin were both standing over him, eager for a fight. The man looked ready to oblige them, then sat back down.

At the bottom of the slope stood the statuesque blond figure of Blythe Northrup. Her long legs were spread in a determined stance. Her long fair hair whipped in the wind. And balanced against her shoulder, she aimed the long barrel of a rifle at the man on the ground.

"Geeze, Blythe," Harry groaned. "You take all the fun out of everything."

Ruskin pulled the Arab man up and handcuffed him. "Looks like you've been watching those war movies with your husband," he said.

Blythe gave him a dazzling smile. "We call it quality time," she purred.

The sound of a car engine turning over sounded loudly back at the house. "Oh, gosh! Sikina's getting away!" Valentina shouted and plunged back up the slope.

Harry was right behind her. "Val!"

The squeal of tires was loud. It echoed a bit off the surrounding cliffs. There followed two distinct sharp blasts of horns. Then the quick whine of a police siren.

Valentina and Harry skidded to a halt at the top of the rise. Down below, three vehicles blocked a fourth from leaving. Gene Beyer's long, cream Caddy had neatly cut Sikina off at one end of the driveway. A black and white police car, its beacon flashing silently, was catty-cornered to it. At the nearest edge of the drive a soft blue stationwagon was parked. Nina Beyer was easing herself from beneath the wheel. Behind her four other eager people spilled out into the road.

"Grandma!" Valentina yelled and took off running.

"Damn," Harry murmured in shock. He was right behind Valentina when she thundered up to the wagon.

Gene Beyer was yelling at his wife. "You were supposed to stay at the motel waiting for a call!" he stormed.

Nina let him rage then wrinkled her nose at him. "And let you have all the fun? When Mrs. Crosby showed up with ..."

"Dad!" Harry clasped one of the new arrivals in a fond hug. Then he turned to the others. "Mom! Pop!"

"... with all of Harry's parents, what could we do?" Nina continued to explain to her husband. "It was Pete's idea that we call the police. Mrs. Crosby called in an old favor to get a squad car immediately. Dawud says he'll take care of Sikina, get her medical help. He's going to urge Badr to divorce her. And, sweetheart, you're just going to love Bunny ..."

Loretta Crosby hugged her granddaughter, squeezed her hands. It was then that she noticed the diamond ring was missing from Valentina's finger.

"I changed my mind," Valentina said. "Just as you hoped I would."

Loretta beamed with approval. "Oh, darling, I'm so glad. I know you won't live as close but you'll be much happier with Harry."

"I'm going to go back to school, too, Grandma. Become an archaeologist."

"Like Dawud al-Bakil," Loretta said. "And like Harry. His father told me about his plans to go into archaeology now, too."

It was only then that Valentina really noticed the three strangers. Behind her Sergeant Cole Ruskin handed over his prisoner to the local police. They already had a very subdued Sikina in the back of the squad car. "Come meet our new family, Val," Loretta urged.

Pete Smith was a raw-boned man. A little shorter than Harry, he had light-brown hair, an easy smile, and a strong handshake. Beside him, his wife, Bunny, was as delicate and fragile as a piece of porcelain. Her fair hair had a number of attractive streaks of silver running through it. But her eyes were as lively and as bright a blue as the cloudless sky overhead. They were Harry's eyes, Valentina realized. Bunny enveloped her in a cloud of tea rose perfume. Her hug was enthusiastic and welcoming.

When she turned to the taller, silent man, Valentina caught her breath a bit. Except for his eyes, the man was an older version of Harry. This hair was sprinkled with gray. Silver touched his temples and colored his close cut beard. "So this is the infamous Valentina," the man said and smiled. His teeth glinted, his ebony eyes twinkled.

Everyone seemed to babble at once. Valentina didn't care. The adventure was over. Sikina and her cohorts had been caught. Back in Yemen, Badr will still missing but she couldn't worry about him. Perhaps he had found the tomb of the Queen of Sheba. Before he left, Harry would give his father the telling section of the map. Dawud could decide whether to recover the artifact hidden in the cache or to leave it hidden. It wasn't going to complicate her life any longer.

Cole Ruskin had joined the group now, explaining how he'd discovered everyone was converging on Las Vegas. Loretta's call telling the Washington police that she was headed there, coupled with Sikina's sudden flight and Harry's steady westward heading had all jelled. He'd placed a few other calls and discovered that Dawud al-Bakil had left Cairo bound for New York and that he'd connected to a flight to Las Vegas as well. "It all had to end here," he explained.

Loretta was just as eager to tell of her adventures. First she'd flown to Salt Lake City and made a connection for the Elko airport. It hadn't taken her long to find Pete and Bunny Smith. She'd been staying at their ranch. After she told them of the two attempts on Harry's life, Bunny had placed a call to Dawud.

"Like a knight errant, he dropped everything to rush here," Loretta enthused. Bunny gave her first husband a smile of glowing admiration. Pete Smith tightened his grip on his wife's hand. Dawud al-Bakil just looked amused.

Valentina looked from one face to another. Denny and Blythe Northrup were full of their own part in the rescue. They were both talking. Gene and Nina Beyer were still arguing. Bunny and Pete Smith had buttonholed Cole Ruskin. Her own grandmother was smiling up into Dawud al-Bakil's handsome face with all the admiration of a star-struck teenager at a rock concert.

"I guess we can't get out of it," Valentina murmured.

At her side, Harry nodded. He stuffed his hands in the pockets of his jeans, afraid he'd ruin the moment if he touched her. "Nope," he agreed. "We're doomed, Val. With the whole family gathered, there's only one question left to ask. When do you want to get married?" He paused a moment, almost holding his breath. She was more precious to him than ever. She'd come to rescue him. Then his lips relaxed into an amused smile.

"Is this afternoon too soon?" he asked.

"Much too soon."

He took a deep breath. "Listen, I know things have been happening fast, Val. But don't you think that after five years you might have an answer?"

Valentina twinkled up at him. There was a smear of dust across her cheek. Her pastel T-shirt advertised the famous Front Street Museum in Dodge City.

Harry pulled his hands out of his pockets and put them on her shoulders. "Do you remember all those historical markers we saw in Oklahoma and Kansas?" he asked. "The ones you looked after so longingly but never uttered a peep about?"

"Oh, those?" Her emerald eyes darkened.

"If you marry me soon, we can go back and honeymoon along the same route. Find new ones. Anything you like Val. And whenever we find one, we'll stop and I'll make love to you."

She moved closer, into his arms.

"Now, Valentina Crosby, will you please marry me tomorrow?" Harry asked.

"*Late* tomorrow," she said. "After all, Harry, I've got to go shopping first!"

He chuckled softly. "For something to wear."

"Oh no. For something far more important. We need a large bottle of vitamin E." At his blank look, Valentina laughed. "Harry. Some of those markers were only a mile apart. You're gonna need a lot of energy!"

Epilogue

ELIOT FARADY WAITED and watched. Badr al-Hashid had stolen from the house at first light. He hadn't even checked behind to see if he was being followed. He just moved steadily up the mountain, taking nearly the same course Faraday had behind Nahar and Mohammad a few days ago. Badr clutched an object to his chest as he walked. Faraday hadn't gotten much of a look at it. Just enough to see that it was wrapped in cloth that sparkled when the early rays of sunlight struck it. Gaudy as the spangled veil of a dancing girl in the bazaar.

Farady closed the distance quickly, afraid that Badr would make it to the entrance and disappear as Nahar had done just days earlier. This time he would be closer, would see where the hidden entrance was located.

Badr reached the ledge and moved along it at a snail's pace, careful never to look down into the gorge below. He wouldn't see, then, the fluttering remains of the two greedy souls who'd traveled that route to Paradise. Perhaps, Faraday mused, he would do as Sikina asked after all. Who was to say if Badr al-Hashid had merely slipped, or if his skull had been crushed before his body plunged off the precipice?

Farady sat in the blind of a scrawny bush and watched through its feathery branches as his unknowing guide searched for the opening.

Badr counted as Nahar had told him, feeling his way along until he reached the special formation. Clever, he thought. Just enough of the rock had been chipped away to form the symbol for her name in the ancient text. The cuts were old and weathered by time as well. But he knew them just as Nahar had known he would. The thief himself hadn't known what the markings stood for, he had merely recognized the stone as a signpost made by man.

Upwards he reached. Ah, it was there. Cleverly disguised. An opening little bigger than a man was wide, sheltered by a large rock, covered by desert growth. It was invisible to the naked eye. Even knowing it was there, Badr could not see inside the cave.

He pulled himself up toward it, maneuvered and dropped through the opening. Gravel slid beneath him, bringing him down the shaft quickly. He lost his footing and thudded into the cave wall. Something rattled and crumbled beneath him. Still clutching the covered plaque to his chest, Badr fumbled in his robe for the flashlight he'd brought along.

A curse rumbled from his thoat. His fall had destroyed the bones of a man, a servant of some kind. Others of his kind lay along the other walls. He counted them. So very few to serve a queen. He surveyed the outer chamber carefully. No markings on the walls. No gathered supplies. The skeletons along the walls were laid out peacefully, dead men before they'd been sealed in the tomb.

In the center of the room the remains of a wooden chair had crumbled beneath yet another dead man. Bands of copper lay among the debris. Cuffs of silver, now blackened with age, still encircled the wrists of the skeleton form. Other silver ornaments lay near. When the wood had at last given way, the man who'd sat in the chair had spilled to the floor. His skull with its gruesome grin faced Badr. The long dead nobleman seemed to be smirking.

It was only a trick of the light, Badr told himself. He turned to trace the rest of the cavern.

He hadn't entered through the main entrance after all. It had once been wide and spacious. Now it was filled with rubble. Nahar had found a weakening in the mountain itself, not a secret doorway. As Badr's light came back around he saw why Nahar had brought him the plaque. It had been the first item the thief had felt upon falling through the roof himself.

Badr peered, nearly breathlessly, through the narrow opening into the inner chamber. The temptation was nearly unbearable. But he would not enter the sacred precinct of the queen yet. Not until he could show the world that he was not the madman some of his colleagues termed him. He had known she existed. From now on every step he took would follow every rule lain down by academia or government. He would guard this find from dispute.

Carefully Badr uncovered the golden plaque and refit it in place, sealing the queen's final resting place once more, if but temporarily.

He was unprepared for the rain of scree that preceded the red-haired man.

"My, my," Faraday smirked. "Not very prepossessing, is it?"

The beam from Badr's flashlight picked up the glint of steel in the American doctor's hand. The muzzle of the gun was pointed at the center of his chest.

"So it was you," Badr rumbled, fury building inside him. They would take his treasure, his perfect find, away from him.

Faraday seemed unaware of his former patient's anger. "In the *suq*? Wouldn't go near the place at night," the doctor claimed. "That was your darling wife, old man. Sweet thing, Sikina. Not terribly bright, of course. But sensual. You were quite right. She is a slut. A very talented one."

The fiery-haired doctor waved the gun. "Show me this treasure. I've been looking for it for days without luck."

Cautious now, Badr motioned to the room within which they stood. "To an archaeologist, there does not have to be gold or jewels to make a find his treasure," he said.

Faraday's eyes narrowed. His slashing brows drew together. "Are your trying to say Sikina tricked me?"

"Tricked? You deceived yourself, seducer of women."

Faraday laughed shortly. "Don't give me all the credit, Hashid. I knew that hot little number you married long before she went to your couch." He glanced around the cave. The glint of gold caught his eye.

The gun wavered again, urging Badr to comply with orders. "Move that light over this way," Faraday said.

Badr did as he was requested and willed the American to forget him. Just for a moment.

"This is more like it," the doctor murmured when the golden plaque was illuminated. "There's writing on it." He turned back to Badr, a smirk still curving his lips. "Your wife tells me you can read this stuff. So what's it say?"

Badr hunkered down, his feet flat, his knees bent. "It is a warning," he said. He ran a hand lightly over the inscription from right to left. "A curse from the mukarrib who guards her."

"A curse." Faraday laughed again. The sound echoed loudly in the small cave. "What 's a mukarrib? Some fanciful creature like a griffin or a phoenix?

"He," Badr said, pointing to the grinning skull, "is the mukarrib." As Faraday's smile widened, Badr shrugged. "It is just an educated guess, of course."

"And he protects who?"

"Queen Bilqis." Badr's voice was very calm. He could have been lecturing to a classroom rather than explaining things to a barbarian in the anteroom of a royal tomb.

"The lady behind door number one," Faraday murmured. "Let's see what surprises she has in store for us, shall we?"

He shoved the gun back into the waistband of his now filthy beige trousers. His fingers curved around the upper corners of the golden plaque.

Badr swung the flashlight, bringing it down smartly against the back of Faraday's skull. The doctor staggered, fell and tried to pull his gun free. Badr was on him, one hand pressing tightly on the American's windpipe, the other grasping Faraday's wrist, turning the gun away. The gun exploded. Beneath him, Badr felt Faraday collapse.

Shaking, the archaeologist backed away from the dying man. He searched in the dark for the flashlight, then watched as the last vestige of life faded from Eliot Faraday's face.

"Desecrator," he hissed at the dead man. "Defiler of tombs."

His voice echoed back to him, sounding unearthly and unlike his own.

He could not have the body of the American in the tomb. He was an anathema to the memory of Bilqis, a blemish that would destroy all that Badr himself had worked for. He would have to drag the body out, drop it over the cliff. All traces that the tomb had been disturbed must be hidden.

The echo still played in his head. "Desecrator. Defiler."

The beam from Badr's flashlight gleamed on the grinning skull of the mukarrib. "*Defiiiilllllleeeerrrrr*," the tomb whispered.

There was a stirring beneath him, as if the mountain itself now picked up the word. It trembled, quivering with fury. And up above, the curse was picked up by the wind, by the sound of rubble gathering, falling, tumbling to answer the last wish of the mukarrib, the guardian of the tomb of the Queen of Sheba.

The dim glow of daylight disappeared beneath the landslide as once more the cave was sealed. The flashlight glowed like a spotlight on the long dead nobleman and the tarnished emblems of his office. Badr al-Hashid was still staring at the skull's self-satisfied smirk when the batteries failed.